THE DILATORY

By Kimberley Dawn

Geoff —
  A fellow Avid reader.
 Hope you enjoy
     Kim ♡

   Kimberley
     Dawn

This book is dedicated to my son, my brother, my childhood companion, my best friend, the love of my life, my black Lab, my B.B., who was with me through good times and bad, always at my side, always loving me, ever faithful.

He had a white blaze on his chest, one white toe, and white hair on one of his feet, so I don't know if he was all Lab, but that was the predominant breed in his genetic makeup and I've heard purebred labs aren't all squat in stature or all black. A lot have white on them. He was taller than a standard Labrador, too, very statuesque. Whatever his DNA, he was the best, bravest, most loving, most loyal, four-legged angel to ever walk this Earth. He taught this little girl at eleven about love and at twenty-six, about loss.

Never in my life have I missed anyone as much as I miss my B.B. I was, and am, honored to have had him in my life. Twenty-six years have passed without him, yet the loss still feels raw and new.

I look forward to holding him on the Other Side.

I also dedicate this to every one of your children, pets, spouses, and all other family members and significant others you've lost. God loves us all, and we'll all be together again like we were never apart. Time goes by so slowly here, and time practically stands still on the Other Side. Fifty years can pass here while we're missing our loved ones, yet it's like a heartbeat over there. There's no such thing as forgetting there.

You, my reader, are loved. You are remembered, as they are by us.

Dilatory

/dil-a-to-ry/

Noun: the curtain raiser

Adjective: slow to act; intended to cause delay

He had been dilatory in appointing a solicitor.

Synonyms: slow, tardy, unhurried, sluggish, lazy

Prologue

Shawna went for a jog near her house. Minutes in, the sun went down, and darkness fell immediately--no sunset, no stars, no moonlight. There was nothing but darkness. She stopped to stretch out a cramp in her leg. Leaning against a tree, she scanned the landscape, trying to get her bearings. She didn't know where she was but didn't think she'd gone too far from home.

Shadows seemed to loom in the darkness. A tree branch suddenly reached out from the trunk of the tree as if it were a twisted limb with claws grasping for something solid to free it from the ground it was embedded in.

She ran in the direction she thought was home, the tree's limbs following her as far as it could reach from its eternal prison. She could feel that she was being followed. Heavy footsteps hit the pavement behind her. She hastened her pace. Her heart beating out of her chest, breathing labored, she turned to see who was behind her. There wasn't just one person, but many people.

She saw a driveway, an escape from the street. It was a means of evading her pursuers, so she didn't care whose property she was on. She had no idea she had just entered the Wainsborough Cemetery or how she had gotten this far from home and why she left without Beau to begin with. Nothing was making sense to her, let alone why there was an angry mob chasing her.

As she ran, she dodged headstone after headstone, one grave marker after another. She thought with all the dodging and weaving in and out of obstacles she had done, surely she would have shaken off her pursuers, but looking out from behind a massive monument with the image of a female angel on top, she saw them still coming.

Shawna crouched down behind the monument, and she was grabbed. She started to scream, but she knew they'd hear her. She thought it couldn't be them already. Had they found her so soon? Hands gripped her ankles. She struggled to get away. Despite her struggle to free herself, the grip tightened. Her feet felt as if they were in shackles. She twisted and turned to no avail. Her phone! Why hadn't she thought of that earlier? She got it out, hit the flashlight icon, shined it toward her feet, and gasped.

Out of the ground, clutching her ankles were two leathery, knobby, skeletal hands. She was panicking, knowing the people were fast approaching, but even more so now. She couldn't believe what she was seeing. All she could do was remain still.

She wanted to scream but didn't want to give away her hiding spot.

As frightened as she was, she had no choice but to crouch there with those grotesque, twisted, icy digits touching her, restricting her movement. She cried. She quivered, terrified and helpless. She could still turn her upper body and look to see how close her pursuers were to what was supposed to be her sanctuary.

She carefully stood and peered around the blockade, bringing herself face to face with a man. She cried harder as he stepped around the headstone. He was hideous, an emaciated, near skeletal version of what was once a human being. He had skin that looked as if it had been dehydrated, sunken holes where eyes once were, and a jaw that hung askew. Shawna screamed. A woman approached, gurgling words, but Shawna couldn't make out what she was saying. The woman was in as bad a shape as the man, and they both smelled of rotting flesh. Others came until she was completely surrounded.

Then she heard the snapping of bones and was jerked downward. She felt her legs being covered in dirt. She shined her flashlight on the ground at her feet again and saw the corpse rising from its grave. It was pulling her down into its sepulcher, its attempt to make her part of the necropolis. She screamed, kicked, and fought like she never had, flaps of cold, wet, necrotic, skin sliding over her own. Shawna punched wildly at the soulless corpse climbing over her. One blow connected, knocking what was left of the flesh on its skull free, and it landed on Shawna's nose and mouth, suffocating her before the dirt she was being pulled into or the corpse crawling over her could. She awoke to Beau licking her face and Kelley rubbing her head where Shawna had hit her. "Shawna, it's me, Kelley! You were having a bad dream."

Chapter 1

Shawna Livingston sat on her porch, looking out onto the little brook in her backyard and listening to it trickle along a path of rocks. She imagined her life having been different. It wasn't that she didn't appreciate everything she had, but there was something missing. If it weren't for Beau, her best friend, son, brother, her black Lab, steadfast loyal companion, sidekick, everything would be a hopeless blur of parties, the scholarship to Princeton, and boys.

Well, Chandler certainly wasn't a boy. At twenty-eight, he was a man. He was a tall, statuesque, Adonis of a man. He had a chiseled chin, muscles all around, and a full, gorgeous head of thick, dark hair. Her mother had always told her that men didn't grow up until they were around forty. She held out hope that her mother was wrong. She knew all men weren't like that, especially not him. He was a friend. She didn't think that was the relationship he wanted with her, though, but that suited her just fine for now. She valued their friendship too much to ruin it with intimacy, anyway.

Shawna decided she'd be intimate with another man *someday*. She had one in mind she had run into and seen lately since they were kids growing up in the same neighborhood. His name was Paul, and they had been friends back then. He was nice, a gentleman, and good looking, too. He fit the bill just fine. He was the exact opposite of Ian.

Ian was the bad-boy type. She'd had enough of them, the idiots with licenses to drive motorcycles. He was immature, rude, and abusive. If it weren't for Chandler finding them one night and stepping between them, she would've been seriously hurt. The guy had been drinking and popping pills when he got mad at her for looking at a man who had made a comment about her. They were outside a local bar called the POP INN. It doubled as a hotel. He got jealous and was in her face, yelling at her nose-to-nose, and he had his hands on her throat. She had merely looked at the man who was addressing her directly--that's it.

Chandler rescued her from that loser and busted him upside his stupid, thick head. *What kind of a man puts his hands on a woman anyway?* she thought.

She reached down and patted Beau on his soft, fuzzy head, but that just wasn't enough. She set her coffee down, pulled him close to her, put her face in his scruff, and kissed him. She said, "You're the only man for me, Beau."

That night at the bar, that jerk Ian had shown how bad he truly was. That was it for him! She wouldn't tolerate any man putting his hands on her. It tainted her view of relationships entirely. A month later, Chandler was still yelling at her for being so foolish as to let that idiot in as far as she had. She had been engaged to him, and she had let him have every inch of her body. Now, she didn't want a boyfriend at all.

After that first serious relationship, she knew she was too guarded to enter into another one beyond friendship. When she and Paul were kids, he was always nice and quiet. And Chandler was too damn good-looking for his own good anyway. When they were out for coffee, girls would stare at him, but he wouldn't pay any attention to them. He seemed to only have eyes for Shawna. One girl even dropped her clutch purposefully so she could bend over in front of him. He could care less about childish, loose girls like that. Ian, on the other hand, would have said something provocative to the girl with Shawna sitting right there. He was an immature pig. She should have known better than to get involved with someone as disrespectful as he was.

After the first night she spent with Ian in his basement apartment, they had gone upstairs for her to leave and meet his parents. When they were up there, he said, "Why don't you comb your hair or something?" And in front of his parents, too! *I bet they were so proud of him for that!* she thought, still petting Beau. *I was good enough for him to take my innocence, though.* He was a despicable excuse of a man, and that was just the beginning of his showing his ignorance.

The best move she ever made was getting away from that loser. If he had known how she cared for her long, curly hair, he'd have known she would never run a comb or brush through it without leave-in conditioner. Actually, she never ran a brush through it, period.

"There's that noise again, Beau." His ears were up, head cocked. She knew he had heard it, too. At least this house wasn't like the old house on Valley Street. That place was clearly haunted. There were so many stories she could tell, but who would believe her other than Chandler and Kelley?

Shawna's majoring in Theology would put her over the top with telling ghost stories as far as her peers were concerned. She knew what she had seen. Besides, every major religion believes the soul survives the physical body's death. They were all too closeminded to understand, she guessed.

Chapter 2

The next morning, her neighbor Jess and his dog Gussy, a sweet basset hound, showed up to say hello. Beau greeted them with his usual enthusiasm. Gussy was a girl, after all. Shawna said, "Hi Jess. Your garden looks beautiful, but I don't see you out there working in it like I have to do with mine every day. How do you do it?"

"I usually work in it later on at night, Missy," he said. "You're probably out galivanting. That's why you don't see me." *Hmph,* Shawna thought. But, far be it for her to be disrespectful to her elders, so she said nothing and only smiled a little while he went on about his gardening techniques.

Shawna glanced about her property. Hers was a grand old home, nothing she'd be able to afford on her own. She wouldn't have it at all if it weren't for her parents having given it to her lock, stock, and barrel before moving to Florida to their summer home. The weather was kinder to her father's arthritis there. Unless health issues affected her, she didn't want to leave this place; there were too many memories. Plus, she had friends here, especially Chandler and Kelley. Besides, she liked the four seasons. New Jersey was like fifteen minutes by train from where she lived. And she lived out in the country, away from the hustle and bustle of New York City. She liked it here, and this is where she'd stay if she could help it.

She appreciated that she didn't have to worry about staying in the dorm any more or renting an apartment near campus, even though Beau was welcomed at both places. There was nothing like the comforts of home. Besides, Beau had his own backyard now with two acres, fenced in, to run and play.

Sometimes she felt guilty that she couldn't enjoy the land with Beau as often as she wanted to. She wasn't home until eight or nine every night after waitressing at the Robin's Nest. Thankfully, though, Chandler helped to keep Beau company. He would stop by the house, pick up Beau, and bring him to meet her for coffee after the lunch rush. When they couldn't meet up, Chandler would stop and play ball with him a couple of times a day, and if he had time and wasn't working, he'd just hang out at her place with Beau all day. He was an unofficial roommate.

Chandler said he'd stay with Beau during her classes, too, so everything worked out for everyone. She wasn't quite sure how he could dog sit and work his nighttime job, but she guessed he took naps at her place. Heaven knows Beau slept half the day away, especially in the winter.

Just as Jess wrapped up some bit of advice about newspapers between garden rows, a rumbling noise sounded from the basement. Beau barked. "Shhh," she said. "Beau, be quiet." Gussy heard it, too. They were on the backyard deck at the patio door when Gussy heard Beau barking and ran in and made a beeline for the basement.

Shawna followed the dogs. Jess trailed after. She thought she saw a lady with short, gray curly hair in a long white gown pass by the door where she thought the noises were coming from in the basement. She didn't say anything about it to Jess, but she saw him looking in that direction, too. *Naturally, anyone who'd have seen that would have said something about it to her, right?* She called Beau and Gussy, but they stood there, heads down, growling.

Jess said he thought it might just be the furnace. "Silly dogs," Shawna answered. "Come on. Let's go back outside."

"I've heard that before, you know, when I used to visit Pearl here when we'd sit in her kitchen, but that was before we had furnaces. That fireplace of yours takes me back. We'd sit in front of it and brew coffee and have the best cornbread from a skillet we'd cook it in."

"Really Jess?" she asked, thinking, Ok old man, you really are losing it.

"Yep! Gussy and me, we were her daily company," he said.

She knew he was off his rocker then because that woman Pearl had died years before her great-grandfather bought the house. Perhaps he was remembering something from his childhood and another dog. She said, "That's a nice memory, Jess. We'll talk about it more when I get back. Could you come by and let Beau out to potty while I'm gone today? I don't know what Chandler's plans are."

Just as Jess said he would, Chandler showed up. "I was just talking about you," she said to Chandler. "I was going to have Jess let Beau out if you weren't going to be around today."

"You know I'm always here for you and Beau, Shawna," he said.

"Okay, I'll be back by nine or ten. Thanks Chand," she said as she grabbed her bag and walked off. As she was leaving, she turned around and said, "There's food in the fridge." She told him to help himself and that he had her number in case he needed to get ahold of her.

She got into her Volkswagen Beetle. She loved her little car. It was deep purple with a light purple leather interior. She had it custom made. Purple is her favorite color. As she backed out of the driveway, a little girl ran behind her car from out of nowhere chasing a ball. "Shit!" She slammed on her brakes. It was the same kid she'd see all alone in the neighborhood at all hours of the day and night. Shawna thought, *Where are her parents?* She'd have to go talk with them about their daughter. ` It's the same girl she saw out after eleven the other night. That's not right! She can't be more than ten! If this continues, she'd have to call the cops! She backed out of the driveway, threw her car in first, and headed out towards the main road.

She enjoyed these drives by herself, especially the area by Dunn's creek, so pretty. It was a curvy kind of steep road with at least a fifty foot drop off. She'd have to be careful in the winter.

People have said the bridge is haunted at the creek. Some kid was driving too fast, and it had been raining, and he skidded out of control and went over the cliff. His car blew up when it hit the jagged rocks below. Whew! Thank goodness for her new snow tires!

Chapter 3

Just then, she saw Andrew. He was one of the locals that spent his time climbing the rocks there. She never saw him at the college. She wondered what he did constructive with his time. She slowed down and asked if he needed a ride, "No thanks. I'm just killing time," he said. She thought, *Must be nice*. She'd love to have that kind of free time to stroll around and check everything out. As a matter of fact, she wanted to climb down and see where the car had crashed. Supposedly, you can see the boy's specter at exactly twelve thirteen a.m. when the train lights hit the spot where his car had crashed.

She'd talk to Chandler, and while she was at it, Andrew too, and see if they wanted to go with her. She hardly ever saw Andrew, except when he was on his walks or climbing the rocks there. She'd bet he'd already been to the spot. He probably started the rumor!

That aside, it was time for her to start thinking about school. She had Theology; Biblical parables and prophecies, first thing with Professor Briggs. He didn't look old enough to be a professor, but his credentials were there on his wall, and her dad knew him. He had spoken highly of the family, especially his father Samuel Briggs whom he knew and was rather fond of.

Her dad and Samuel used to take the catamaran out on the bay and whale watch in the spring. They sailed and fished too, and were good at telling big fish stories. She imagined they drank their fair share of brandy while they were at it, and that helped embellish their stories of "the big one" that got away. She smiled at that thought. Her dad had left the vessel for her. It was docked at the harbor at Witcham Bright.

Old Dan Sawyer took great care of her. Every time she referred to the vessel as an "it", he corrected her and said it was a "her." It had been awhile since she'd been out there sailing. Daddy paid for "her" to be docked out there, and she hadn't taken her out since last summer with that idiot Ian Steele. Her father didn't like him one bit, and that's probably why she had given him a chance to begin with.

Her father had, had her whole life planned out for her. She'd go to Princeton. After all, she was a legacy. She'd marry Sloane and Jerry Paxton's son Jerrod, who was following in his father's footsteps, majoring in medicine. She'd have the house, the three kids, the dog, the cat, the white picket fence, and she'd never have to worry about money, because Daddy would pay for her books for school, and she'd have an allowance of four thousand a month until she could access her trust fund when she was twenty-seven. That seemed an odd age to her to access a trust fund. All of her friends had already gotten theirs at the age of twenty-five. Either way, she told her dad that she didn't like Jerrod Paxton and she'd pay for her own books, gas and what not for school.

But it had been a struggle, even with not having to pay the utilities or anything on the house. Her father made sure everything was paid for down to the property taxes and maintenance workers for her home. Groceries were sent to her home weekly by an account her mom had set up for her before they left town. She sure didn't mind that. Mom always knew what she liked to have around the house to eat and cook. Her mom was an awesome cook and baker. Shawna had learned from the best.

After Shawna's first class, she'd have Trigonometry, Calculus, and her elective, Latin, and then lunch in the cafeteria with Kelley. It looked more like a food court in a mall than a school cafeteria, college or not. She could eat at work too if she wanted to, but this way she could spend time with Kelley. Then, home to change and shower, and see Beau for a couple of hours, then back to work until eight or nine. Then, home again to sleep with Beau. She couldn't wait to snuggle up to him and smell his fuzzy head. There was nothing better than coming home to him and a cup of hot cocoa with whipped cream or an ice-cold glass of milk with lemon sandwich cookies. She could taste them now.

The lunch crowd was annoying to the point that she was ready to stop working the split shift and just work the dinner shift through the week. She'd still do the split shift on weekends. Two days were more tolerable than seven in a row of that craziness. That would free up some of her time.

She loved it here in Spring Lake, but didn't know how a career as a Theologian would pan out in this little town. She'd swing by the beach on her way home and head to Witcham Bright and take the April Colleen out for a sail. Chandler wouldn't mind her being a little late. After all, he had everything he could ask for at her house except her there. Beau was great company though.

Chapter 4

Kelley Audair had awoken with a start from a horrible dream she had that morning. In it, she saw her friend being chased and assaulted in a cemetery, but she couldn't help her. Her roommate Megan Franco was sitting up looking at her with disbelief.

"Who's Shay?" Megan asked.

"Why?"

"Because you were yelling that name in your sleep half the night! I was up cramming for tests last night and as soon as I got to sleep, your screaming woke me back up again."

"Sorry about that, Meg. I had a dream about my best friend Shawna. I call her Shay sometimes."

Megan scowled. "Sounded more like a nightmare to me."

Kelley shrugged. "Like I said, sorry."

Megan huffed and stormed into the bathroom with a towel slung over her shoulder. Kelley heard cabinet doors and drawers opening and closing as Megan rifled through her belongings. The sound of the shower head followed. Kelley sighed and rolled her eyes. *Let's hope a hot shower calms her down,* she thought. Just seconds later, a sudden gasp sounded from behind the bathroom door. The water shut off.

"Meg?" Kelley asked, tapping lightly on the door.

"Great!" Megan boomed as she tore open the door, still dressed in her pajamas. "Now I'm seeing things."

"You're seeing things?"

"Never mind, Kelley," she said, tearing clothes out of her closet. "I don't have time to shower anyway. And I'm sure I'll ace these tests today, so thanks for that."

"What did you see?" Kelley's head spun while she watched Megan -moving through the apartment like a tornado.

"Nothing."

"Meg, what was it?"

"Kelley! I don't have time for this. We're the only ones here. There's no reason for someone else to be standing in our shower, right? See? Hallucinations brought on by sleep deprivation, all thanks to you." Without another word, Megan threw her bag over her shoulder and stomped out of the apartment, slamming the door behind her.

When she was sure Megan was out of earshot, Kelley entered the bathroom, her attention on the shower curtain. "Hello?" she said. The curtain ruffled but no voice sounded and she went about her morning routine.

Dressed and ready, Kelley left the apartment and found other girls standing in groups of two or three in the hallway. They were all whispering and staring. Kelley only smirked at the sight of a cluster of menacing spirits surrounding the girls. One in particular, a strikingly thin male figure, was walking so close to the head bitch of the bunch that for a split second, Kelley considered intervening, but it was a fleeting thought. She wouldn't listen to Kelley anyway, so there was no use in trying to convince her that she had an attachment.

She also wondered if Jasmine Dupree had told her boyfriend Carlos that she screwed his best friend when he was off on holiday last year, or if the other girls noticed that Miranda Cole was wearing her lipstick extra thick and more around the outside of her lips to hide that "cold sore" she had gotten when she was gone skiing last winter and ran into Buffy Richter's boyfriend Matt Chambers on the slopes. Miranda went back to "grab a cup of cocoa" with him while her family kept skiing.

The bitches could talk smack if they wanted, but Kelley knew more about them than they thought. She passed Buffy in the hall just then. She found it funny that Ms. Au natural, I-don't-need-makeup-because-I-fake-bake-don't-eat-anything-but-lettuce-or-you'll-gain-an-ounce-girl would suddenly be wearing color on her lips. She looked sickly to Kelley, as if a strong gust of wind would blow her over. Kelley smiled at her and said, "That color looks nice on you, Buffy." Buffy tilted her face downward and tucked her hair behind her ear.

Those girls were all part of the sorority that Kelley wanted nothing to do with. She wasn't like them at all. They had no clue what loyalty as a friend meant. Kelley didn't think any of them were even friends with each other; they were just competition.

Kelley was sick of the roommate life and was ready to get her own place near school. She even considered asking Shawna if she could stay with her. Shawna was cool. She wasn't like the girls here at all. They hit it off the moment they met at the library in high school when Kelley had transferred in, and they had been best friends for the past ten years. Shawna knew of Kelley's abilities and thought it was cool that she had them.

Just then, a girl named Roberta McBirty approached Kelley. From what Kelley could gather, Roberta was a kind and unassuming girl, nothing like the others. As a matter of fact, the other girls made fun of her, too. They called her Birdy.

"You're Kelley, right?" she asked.

Kelley nodded.

"I know you're like me," Roberta said.

"What do you mean?"

"I can see your inner light. I've had this attachment for almost a year now and wondered if you could help me. There's a girl here who claims she's a witch and hexed me."

"That's Kat from the 'popular girls,'" Kelley said. "I think she's full of it, Roberta. She's a witch, alright, but not the cauldron-stirring, potion-brewing kind that people think of."

"How do you know?"

"I really don't, but I'm assuming she's just being mean like the rest of them. I will tell you that there are no such things as curses, so you don't have to worry about that. And I don't see anyone around you, so there's no attachment, either."

"But I have so many issues in my dorm right now, Roberta said, "and I've seen something there every day since I moved in."

"Show me."

In Roberta's dorm, Kelley saw a female spirit immediately. Roberta saw her too. After a brief conversation with the apparition, Kelley learned that it was a girl who used to attend the university and was hazed into drinking too much alcohol, causing her death. The girls responsible for pressuring her had hidden their part in her death. Roberta had the girl's former room.

"How long have you had this room, Roberta?" Kelley asked as the apparition sat on Roberta's' bed.

"For about a year." Pointing at the spirit, Roberta said, '' I started seeing her the first night I moved in. She doesn't talk to me though" The spirit sneered at Roberta.

"I have a solution. My roommate doesn't want to room with me anymore. Why don't you move in with me? She can have your room."

"Are you sure you want to go to all that trouble?"

Kelley nodded. "It's no trouble. You're doing me a favor."

"Thank you," Roberta said.

"This apparition isn't ready to cross over yet, so it looks like Megan will have a built-in roommate. We'll see who she thinks is crazy now." Kelley winked exaggeratedly before clapping her hands together once. "I'll help you pack."

A half hour later, Kelley and Roberta trudged across campus with two large, cardboard boxes and a fluorescent orange tote carrying all of Roberta's belongings. At the entrance to Kelley's building, the bitches were huddled in a tight cluster. "Freaks," one of them said." The rest of them snickered.

Kelley snapped her head in the direction of the girl who said it. She was ready to bust her in the mouth. Something in Kelley's eyes must have communicated her position on the matter because the girl closed her mouth and took a half step away from the door, giving Kelley and Roberta plenty of room to get in.

In the apartment, Kelley said, "This is my bed. That will be yours." She pointed to Megan's twin bed decorated with a watercolor floral comforter. "Megan just doesn't know it yet."

"Are you sure this is okay?"

"Trust me. She wants out."

The two sat on the end of Kelley's bed. "So, you said you saw my inner light?" Kelley asked, one eyebrow raised. "How long have you had the sight, and why did you think I could help you?"

Roberta shrugged. "I can just tell there's something special about you. I've been able to see things since I was little. I've always known when something bad was going to happen before it did, who was calling on the phone before I answered, and who was at the door before I opened it." Roberta popped the lid off her tote and began to sort piles of her clothes.

"Sounds like we have a lot in common. Have you ever looked into Wicca?"

Just then, Megan burst into the room. "I thought we agreed that we would check with each other before we invited people over," she said, eyeing Roberta.

Kelley stood. "Can you sit down so we can talk for a second?"

Megan noticed Roberta's pile of clothes and the two boxes lying along the wall. She turned to Kelley with a sneer. "That was fast," she said, sounding almost as evil as one of the bitches.

"Roberta's dorm room is empty now. We'll just touch base with her R.A. and let her know that you two have switched."

Megan snorted and turned on her heel. Just before the door slammed behind her, she said, "I'll be back for my things when *you're* not here. Freak."

"Anyway," Kelley said, but before she could continue, a thought occurred to her. She worried that Megan's soon-to-be roommate apparition may mistake her for one of the sorority girls who caused her death. She stood and ran to the door.

"Megan!" she called.

"What do you want, Freak?" Megan said without turning around.

Kelley blinked and straightened her shoulders. "I'll be leaving around dinnertime tonight. That would be a good time for you to come pack up." At that, Kelley turned around and went back to her apartment, thinking, *Enjoy your ghost.*

Chapter 5

Out on the water, there was such peace. No books, no schedules, no gabby friends—just the easy slapping of the water against the sides of the boat and the sound of the sail moving with the wind. There was just enough wind for an easy sail where Shawna could sit in the cockpit and look at all the houses on the shore.

This was much better than a traditional sailboat. It provided her all of the comforts of home except Beau. No place was home without him. She had a fridge and a dry storage cabinet stocked with all the adult beverages a person could need. She hadn't used it in such a long time that she didn't have it stocked with ice, water, food, or milk. Had she done that, she could have prepared anything on this boat. She loved the idea of calling Chandler and Kelley and having them bring Beau and just taking off for a while, leaving her worries behind, but she couldn't blow school off.

There was only this year and next to finish, and she'd have her degree. Then she just might take everyone on vacation.

Shawna realized how far she'd gone while daydreaming. She was on the other side of the island, and time had gotten away from her. This side of the shoreline had all the huge houses, but there was one that was dwarfed by the opulent mansions. It was too cute, too quaint, to be where it was. She thought it must have been the only original home there, and all the huge homes must have been built around it. She would choose that place over any of those enormous ones. Bigger wasn't always better. It was the only one that looked like it belonged there. She loved it. She decided she'd have to go see the inside of it someday soon.

Behind her, she heard what sounded like feet sloshing in wet shoes as they were dragged along the deck. She turned to see what the noise was and saw nothing. She thought she might have a stowaway seal aboard, but since there was none to be seen, she assumed the noise was the result of the constant rubbing of the line on the sail. She checked the line, but it hadn't been chafing. She disregarded the noise as a swooshing in her ears with the wind blowing the sail.

As the sun had begun to set, admiring the view, Shawna felt an eerie sensation that had crept over her. She felt as if she weren't alone and resolved to head home.

Shawna made it back to the harbor in forty-five minutes. Dan happened to be standing there, watching and waiting for her to dock. She eased the vessel into place, "coming abreft of the dock," as Dan had once told her. She threw him one rope and jumped onto the dock with the other rope in her hand.

"How was it today?" Dan asked.

"Beautiful," she said, tying the rope to the pier.

Chapter 6

Thursdays were Shawna's favorite days. Class ended early, and she had the night shift off. This was her time to relax. She pulled into her driveway, and Beau trotted toward her, his otter-like tail swinging back and forth. Chandler was behind him. *Damn*, she thought. Much of his chest was showing from beneath a loosely tied white shirt. With it, he wore jeans and boots. The sun hit him with all the colors of the rainbow, like he was wading in water. Light reflected blindingly from a silver medallion that hung from his neck. She shielded her eyes.

Chandler smiled welcomingly and reached around Beau, who had already taken his place on Shawna's lap, to lift her bag of books from the passenger seat. He offered his other hand to Shawna. He smelled of cookies.

"Hey," she said, taking his hand. That was her greeting for everyone. Her mother didn't like that kind of "hello" one bit. Her frequent retorts included, "Hey, what?" or "Hay's for horses."

"Did you eat the roast beef in the fridge?" she asked him as she stood.

"Beau and I made short work of it," he said. "Thanks."

"Do you have enough room left over for dinner? Kelley's coming over, and I always make enough for a crowd."

"Depends on when you two eat," he answered. I've got to get down to the marina. I told Dan I'd help him with something. And I have to work tonight."

"Dressed like that?" She raised an eyebrow and exaggeratedly scanned him from his face to his feet and back again.

"What do you mean? I'm wearing jeans."

"Well, you make them look very nice."

"You're biased."

"Yep."

Beau followed the pair into the house, his tail wagging. He was wearing his usual doggy grin, though he had not yet received his typical greeting from Shawna. She realized this before long and bent down to hug and kiss the fuzzy head of her forever friend. "I missed you, too, baby," she said. "Speaking of Kelley coming over," she said, still flopping Beau's ears, "she's got a huge crush on you."

"She's nice, but no thanks." Chandler took a seat at the kitchen table. "She's a little off, don't you think?"

Shawna paused, then said, "Well, she does think of herself as a white witch, and she claims to see ghosts just about every time

I'm with her. I guess she would 'seem off' to anyone who doesn't know her like I do. Maybe just a little bit."

He shrugged. "Besides, you're the only woman for me, Shawna."

"You know I'm not looking for that kind of relationship." She took a seat across from Chandler. "You're the only man I'll let in as far as I have, but Beau's my main man. I never want another relationship after that douchebag Ian, not that you're not the perfect guy. You are. You're too perfect! You'd never do or say anything that he did to any woman. You know I love you, but as a friend, my best guy friend." She sighed.

"I understand. I value our friendship, and I don't need anything more than that. I said you were the only woman for me because I feel the same way as you do about intimate relationships. You and I are just fine the way we are." He leaned forward onto his elbows and lowered his voice slightly. "I'm glad we're in agreement, yet somehow, I'm disappointed at the same time." He laughed and leaned back again. "Come on funny girl. Let's go see if we have company out back."

Shawna, Chandler, and Beau headed out there to see if Jess and Gussy were working on the garden. "Must be too warm for him today," Chandler said when they saw that Jess and Gussy were not outside. "I'll go check in on him."

Meanwhile, Shawna decided she would check in with Kelley to see when she would be coming over. She sat on the patio and dialed Kelley's number. The call went to voicemail, but as soon as Shawna set her phone down, Kelley called back.

"Don't hate me, but I can't come tonight," Kelley said. "I might be able to make it this weekend, though."

"Kelley…" Shawna grumbled exaggeratedly into the phone. "You better have a good reason." Shawna knew that whatever was keeping Kelley from coming over must have been important because she wouldn't miss a chance to see Chandler if she could help it.

Chandler rounded the corner of the house and sat beside Shawna.

"I do, and I promise I'll tell you all about it this weekend, okay?"

"Worst. Friend. Ever." Shawna said dramatically.

"I know! Write it on my gravestone. I'll call you tomorrow, okay?"

Shawna chuckled and turned to Chandler. "Looks like it's just you and me."

He grinned.

Chapter 7

Across town in New York City, Cora Mae Simms awoke to an acrid smell in her bedroom. She sat up in bed, reached for her glasses, and stood on cracking knees.

Not only did she have dry mouth from smoking a late-night cigarillo, but she also felt parched from the nervousness coursing through her. That smell made her think of none other than Satan himself. She reached for her bedside Bible and clutched it to her chest.

Cora lumbered into her kitchen, grabbed her broom as protection, and went in search of the source of the smell, her callused feet aching with every step. She reached the entrance to her basement and froze, mouth hanging open.

"Lord, help me." She traced the cross over her chest. "He's a bad man." She backpedaled for several steps, then turned and jogged toward her bedroom as fast as her joints would allow. Bible in hand, she prayed. She knew fleeing from something sinister only gave it more power. She had to face her fears, like standing up to a schoolyard bully. "Show you got some backbone," her Auntie Mae used to tell her.

Cora recalled how her Auntie would go to school for her and address the issue of bullying with the principal of Washington High. "My baby" this and "my baby" that was what Cora remembered about the conversations she was made to sit and hear as she waited for her Auntie to walk her home, while all along, her bullies, especially Regina Jackson, waited to pummel her after school. They sat there in the hallway listening to Cora's Auntie yell at the principal about these children. She heard her Auntie call them heathens, and Cora couldn't help but smile at that.

Cora had a bladder control problem that would only be alleviated by an operation. She knew it wasn't her fault, and she knew her Auntie couldn't pay for it at the time, either. Going through school with bullies calling her "piss pants" was hard.

She shook off that memory as her bedroom door squeaked open. "Shag, is that you?" She looked and saw her nondescript fifteen-year-old ball of fur lying in the same spot next to her bed he occupied every night while she slept. If he could still hear, he might be able to defend his mistress, but good ole Shag was deep into his slumber, kicking his geriatric feet and whimpering.

It seemed to Cora he was chasing rabbits in his sleep. That fleeting thought normally put a smile on her face, but now, she was terrified. Her companion, her protectorate, wasn't waking up to defend his home, and more importantly, his human and himself.

The figure came toward her. Cora's bladder released; her Depends underwear were unable to contain the amount that had come from her, and the fluid trickled down her leg as her head was suddenly torn from her body. Her head rolled down to the floor, bounced, and came to a stop in front of her faithful companion while he kept dreaming of rabbits, squirrels, and field mice.

The eyes in Cora's bodiless head blinked once in unmistakable horror as it was nose to nose with her slumbering dog. Her headless body slowly fell to the floor in a loud thud.

The figure turned toward the dog, whose screams were heard down the block. Mr. Jones, one of the only neighbors in the area, heard it and said, "That dog must have gotten himself a fox."

Down the street from where Cora's lifeless body lie and portions of her dog's body were strewn across the house, Dan Wexler left his house smiling, chalking up another conquest he had taken advantage of with crack cocaine. You see, no one could resist his charms when he had a pipe in his hand. That was the only way he could ever get laid. He had no knowledge of a woman's body or how to handle it, much less the equipment to work with. He had what the guys in the locker room back in high school called a baby dick.

He got into his van thinking how he'd tell the story of this dumb bitch to all his guy friends. Did she beg for his cock? Did she suck it until it was so long and hard that he almost couldn't contain his wad before she stuck it in her gushing hole?

He knew that women had holes that needed filling and that he would be the one to do just that to as many as he could lure into his house and bed with that drug. He was into S and M. He was short, balding, and impotent, save for dominating women with drugs and beating them with his whip after they were rendered compliant.

This little girl of thirteen from the neighborhood, Missy Shaver, was a hot ticket to him. He'd lure her into the house with his new puppy. He smirked at the thought of his plan, but his smile faded when he realized he'd have to let the damn thing outside and eventually buy it food.

The little girl could give him some pointers on how to care for dogs since she had two big Alsatian's herself. Yeah, that would be the lure for her.

Maybe she'd like a little booze, maybe a hit from the pipe. Yeah, then he'd have her!

Her dad wasn't home yet, so he wouldn't see where she had gone to. Maybe he could catch her before school.

Sitting at the wheel, Wexler decided he'd have to get back in the house and grab that old whore from last night and get her home so he could focus on the kid. When he was sure no one was around, he headed for the door. His drug-induced paranoia was immense. He was used to the feeling, but he knew he would have to bury it to get the girl.

A foul smell wafted from his bedroom. "Did you just take a shit in my house?" he called around the corner. "Did you miss the fucking toilet?"

The woman rounded the corner. She was taller than he'd remembered. He liked to get them short and small—easier to handle that way. If they weren't weak, he didn't want them.

The woman seemed to be watching her own feet as she approached him: left, right, left. Just steps from him, she stopped.

"Look at me!" Wexler boomed.

She laughed a baritone laugh not her own, her greasy hair hanging in her face. Still facing the floor, she said, "Nunc mea es" *(You're mine now)*.

"What'd you say, bitch?" He cocked his head to the side.

She screamed and flailed her arms, scratching, clawing, digging in a whirlwind of hatred until there was nothing left of Dan Wexler but his "baby dick." She picked the bloody nub off the floor and tossed it to the puppy in the cage before falling to the floor.

The woman regained consciousness hours later only to find herself part of a crime scene investigation. She remembered nothing.

Chapter 8

On that same side of town in New York, away from the peace and tranquility of Spring Lake, a man named Jasper Rawlins was collecting pop cans and any scrap of aluminum he could find on the corner of Forty-Second and Vine when he was approached by a woman who told him to follow her to the back alley. There she stood in the buff after she removed her coat, despite the cold, blustery night. She was young and fresh.

Jasper wiped his mouth on his ragged coat sleeve, his unshaved chin catching on the sleeve of the torn sweater he wore underneath. He spit to rid his mouth of any remnants of chewing tobacco. He spit again, this time into his hands, and slicked back the tufts of hair. He took a step forward.

The young woman didn't run from him, even when he grinned with what few teeth he had left, blackened from years of neglect.

He figured this was his chance to give it to her, right then and there by the dumpster.

Maybe she was one of those kinky broads he had read about back in the day when he was in the service. One horny bitch liked it in the barn in front of the animals, another in the back of a taxi. There were so many kinks he couldn't remember them all.

He inhaled the woman's floral scent, sailing toward him on the midnight gusts that tossed her dark hair about her face.

He felt like a moth drawn to the flame, a fly headed for a spider's web, but he couldn't stop himself from walking toward her. The pull was so great, the allure too enticing.

He buried his doubt and grinned again, satisfied at how easy he knew this conquest would be. There would be no forcing her to have sex with him. This would make one hell of a story for the guys at Tin Pan Alley. He'd embellish the story with as many details he could while they warmed their hands around the fire.

The woman turned around and bent slightly. Jasper dropped his trousers and entered her. She suddenly threw her head backward and spun, and the look of horror on old Jasper's face was cemented there for eternity as he fell to the ground in pieces. First his member, then each arm, his head, torso, and the rest of his bottom half collapsed in a bloody heap. All he had heard was the scythe's blade making its first cut that rendered him incapable of using his pitiful little penis or any other part of his body anymore.

Chapter 9

Kathy Newman staggered out of bed barely able to breathe. She was sure she was misdiagnosed at the clinic the day before but got an antibiotic nonetheless since the doctor knew she had "junk" in her lungs. It wasn't pneumonia, the doctor had said, but dirty, dark mucous from years of smoking cigarettes. The illness going around didn't help. She had an ear infection too, so a broad-spectrum antibiotic was ordered for her.

Kathy justified her tobacco use as a means of increasing her metabolism since she had trusted a doctor to operate on her brain to clip aneurysms and was given a stroke during the surgery. She was now incapable of working, she couldn't use her right arm, and she could hardly walk.

She was susceptible to a myriad of illnesses thanks to the stroke, and she had the people who had beaten her on the head outside of a grocery store on Main for a measly twenty dollars to thank for it all. They had shot her after they got her money from her, but it wasn't fatal. She had had to undergo spinal surgery to remove the bullet, further limiting her mobility. She wished they would have just finished her off instead of leaving her in this condition. Both the spinal cord injury and the stroke made her not want to wake up every night she went to bed. She had been through grueling physical therapy, as well as occupational therapy and was sick of it all. The people there were way too cheerful and at the same time not educated enough in their profession, as far as Kathy was concerned. Aside from that, the particular facility Kathy attended ran through more occupational therapists than she'd imagine any other place would have. Every session she had with a new therapist was an hour-long question-and-answer session instead of time spent helping her to get the use of her arm back. She was sure to tell every one of them what she thought of their lack of professionalism and her own wasted time. Then there was the money.

Kathy did benefit from the physical therapy, though, and she was walking again, if you could call it walking. But at least there were no more wheelchairs or walkers—an occasional use of her cane, but that wasn't so bad considering all she'd been through. She wished Frank would have been there with her that day. His presence there might have deterred the robbers. Either way, according to the doctor, the lung x-ray didn't reveal pneumonia and the nasal swab didn't indicate the flu so she figured she might have another decade of this misery until she would go home again and be healthy, happy and whole once more.

She woke up that morning after a fitful, restless sleep, feeling like she couldn't breathe. Damp from another night of post-menopausal sweating, she did her best to dress with her right leg sliding on her wooden floor. She dressed in the same clothes she wore the night before, foregoing a shower because she was ill and had showered the night before. She wasn't going to see anyone but Frank, and honestly, who cared what he thought anyway? Twenty years ago, yes, she would have jumped right in the shower and gotten all spiffed up, but now, after years of being with him, she was just biding her time with this man until the reaper came for her.

Kathy took an antibiotic and settled in with a cup of joe, a smoke, some Advil, and a date with the toilet. She had been taking stool softeners like they were going out of style since she was started on it in the hospital. Her body had become used to it over the years. She could drink two capfuls and sleep without having to use the toilet until the morning while any other person who drank even one capful would have been running to the nearest bathroom within fifteen minutes of drinking the stuff. Her colonoscopy had been scheduled for the following Monday but was postponed when she had called asking about her use of the antibiotic and they had heard how sick she was over the phone.

Kathy heard a noise behind her while she stirred her coffee in the kitchen. It seemed to be coming from her basement, whose door was adjacent to the entry door of the house. Company this early was uncalled for, so she assumed the sound hadn't been someone knocking.

As a matter of fact, Kathy's being awake this early wasn't right, either, but being as ill as she had been for as many years seemed to throw her internal clock out of whack. It wasn't unusual for her to wake up for the day at midnight. Her routine was hardly "normal," especially since the menopause. She couldn't attribute hearing noises to that, though. That would just be wishful thinking.

Should she call the police? That last one who was out to the house was a real jerk, an Officer McKirty. He was a rookie who thought the badge made his balls bigger according to her neighbor, Mr. Finch. She could see why Mr. Finch thought so. The officer had an air about him, a sort of bravado that was off-putting to say the least. Still, putting up with a "kid' with a badge would be worth the peace of mind she needed now since she was alone and afraid that there was an intruder in her home.

Kathy was sure the police were sick of calls from that neighborhood. It certainly wasn't like it used to be when she was a kid growing up there. She made her way to her phone, grabbed the receiver, dialed, and suddenly saw what was making the noise in her basement. She screamed and dropped the phone, along with her arm, her hand still clutching the receiver. The rest of her body followed soon after, landing on the phone and muffling the voice on the other end, saying, "Nine-one-one, what's your emergency? Hello? Nine- one-one. Do you need help? Can you hear me? Can you speak?"

Chapter 10

The next day in Spring Lake, Shawna was driving off to school. She waved to Andrew, but he didn't see her. He looked as if he were lost in thought as he walked to the edge of the cliff and climbed down onto the rocks. She pulled over to talk to him, but when she looked over the edge, she couldn't find him. She grunted to herself and shrugged. With as many times as he had climbed there, she knew he couldn't have fallen. He must have been tucked beneath a jutting rock.

She thought Andrew must be one of those guys who goes to that new place near Witcham Bright where they climb those man-made rock walls. She wasn't into that—not that she was a girly girl, but it wasn't her thing.

Still concerned, Shawna drove off, looking in her rearview mirror, cussing under her breath. She pulled out onto the highway. "Stupid guy!" she said. "You'd think he'd find something constructive to do with his time. Plant a tree, Andrew! Join the cleanup crew along the highway, something other than climbing those damn rocks." She wondered if he lived down there. *Oh, no! Maybe he's homeless! He's always alone. I wonder if he's eating right?* she thought. *No wonder he's always in those same clothes.* Now she felt bad. She checked the time again in the car. She had a slow start getting out of the house this morning when Jess and Gussy kept her longer than she should have stayed talking about that old lady he used to visit in her house again.

Jess was off his rocker, but he was a sweet old man, a friend she loved. And she and Beau adored Gussy. They were always welcomed at her house. Gussy is such a great pup. She and Beau just love each other. They had pretty much grown up together. After all, Jess had been next door as long as she could remember.

She was just a little girl when he popped over with Gussy and introduced himself to her when she had been playing by the creek. She remembered him calling it a "crick" and talking about there being gold in "that there crick." She had spent the whole summer out there looking for that gold. Either he had been pulling her leg, or he was senile way back then, too.

She wondered how old he was. She guessed eighty or so, but if he knew that old lady who lived in her family home passed down from her Great Grandpa, to her Granddad to Daddy, then that would make Jess at least two hundred, right?

Jess's stories were always interesting. They reminded her of Civil War times she had read about in history class back in high school. Jess knew Granddad well, too. As a matter of fact,

Granddad talked of Gussy, too. She thought that dog must be ancient. Beau must have grown up alongside an already-adult Gussy. Her Great Grandpa used to talk of a man and his dog next door, but she had always assumed that it had been someone else.

Shawna's train of thought suddenly snapped back to Andrew, and she decided that she would bring him some homemade beef stew. She could make a mean stew. That was one of her favorite recipes she had learned how to make from her mom. She planned to stop by the Grab-N-Go after her classes and make some tonight. She'd cook it this evening, reheat it tomorrow, and bring it in the afternoon.

Maybe he wasn't homeless, though. Maybe he was just like all the other guys around town, the thrill seekers, the adrenaline junkies. *That's probably all there is to it*, she thought, tapping her finger absently to the beat of a song on the radio.

But what single guy wouldn't appreciate a homemade meal? Her swinging thoughts were beginning to exhaust her, and she convinced herself to put Andrew out of her mind long enough to concentrate on school.

Chapter 11

Shawna pulled into the parking lot and saw Kelley's car. It stuck out like a sore thumb against the regular cars with its bright pink paint job and all the bumper stickers about flower power and animal welfare. There was no spot close to her car, but Shawna found one five rows back, threw it in neutral, set the parking brake, grabbed the stone Kelley left in her car, and put it in her pocket. Books in hand, she headed to class. She spotted Kelley by the trophy case near her first class.

"Here it is, Kelley." Shawna handed her the crystal. "It's one of yours, right?"

"Nope, but wish it was. It's selenite, and a very beautiful one at that."

"What's selenite?"

"It's a crystal that's referred to as 'liquid light.' It's supposed to have healing powers."

"I do like it, but I can't imagine how it got in my car if it's not yours."

"Keep it. It might bring you luck," Kelley said.

"Are you coming over tonight?" Shawna asked, tucking the stone into her pocket.

"Are you kidding? Do I look stupid enough to pass up a slumber party with Hottie at your place?"

Shawna giggled and headed toward the lecture hall. She stopped in the doorway when she saw that no one else was there yet. She had her crystal clutched in her hand still inside her sweatshirt pocket. She didn't know why, but she felt comforted holding it. She likened the comfort she felt from it to holding a stress ball.

A woman walked into the classroom. Shawna raised an eyebrow at the woman's appearance. She had her hair pulled back in a tight bun. She wore a long-sleeved shirt with a high-collared neck, and she had a skirt on that touched the floor. She wore a shawl over her shoulders, too. At her neckline, she wore a brooch that resembled Shawna's mom's cameo, one she found by her dresser one night when she had dropped her own earring and almost lost it down the heating vent. The woman had a haughty look.

She took her place at the podium, started thumbing through the professor's notes, and looked up at Shawna. Shawna looked around behind herself. She assumed the new professor wanted her to take her seat, so she did. The woman walked up to the chalkboard and wrote on it. She turned around and gave Shawna a menacing look. Shawna shrunk in on herself. The board read, D-I-L-A-T-O-R-Y. While she was no English professor, she was well versed in the English language. She frowned. *I'm not late!* she thought. *This old bat is crazy.*

The woman walked out as the regular professor was walking in. By this time, Shawna was up by the faculty entrance. Her professor spotted her immediately.

"Ms. Livingston, you gave me a start," Professor Briggs said. "You're early. Are you in that great a hurry to do your studies that you'd beat your professor to class?" He opened his briefcase and began to shuffle through paperwork.

Shawna looked down at her wrist, but she had forgotten to put her watch on that morning. "No. Well, yes," she said. "I was running late when I left this morning."

"Late? Not for class. You're actually a few minutes early. I'd imagine the others will be trickling in here momentarily, but I'm glad you're so conscientious of your scheduled studies." He nodded toward the chairs. "Have a seat anywhere, as always."

She picked a seat up front and looked up at the chalkboard. The woman's writing was gone. Professor Briggs hadn't erased anything on the chalkboard yet that she had seen. She raised her hand, but Professor Briggs didn't look up. She cleared her throat loudly.

"Yes?" he asked.

"Can you tell me who that woman was, the one who was leaving when you came in?"

"I'm not sure who you mean," he said, still straightening his notes. "I didn't see anyone here, apart from you, of course."

Shawna huffed quietly and leaned back in her seat. *Why does no one pay attention to what's going on around them?* she thought. She took a notebook and a pen from her bag. *This guy wouldn't see a brick wall two feet in front of him.* She waited for class to start as one by one, students arrived.

After class, Shawna nearly exploded into the hallway, eager to find Kelley and tell her what had happened. She bumped a young man with the door.

"Excuse me," she said.

The young man gave a slight nod. He was in a group of people who must have been running a dress rehearsal for the spring musical. They certainly weren't dressed for a normal day of classes. They didn't look very comfortable, either.

Kelley rounded a corner. "Hey, Kel!" Shawna waved.

"Hey ya, Shay. Isn't this tragic?" Kelley was standing in front of that same trophy case again, this time examining its contents. There was a picture of a woman who had graduated valedictorian and went on to teach at the college there and had passed away in nineteen twelve. Shawna dressed conservatively when the occasion called for it, but the high-collared, Victorian-looking outfit the woman in the photo wore was not a good look. The tight bun didn't help. And why didn't anyone ever smile in pictures back then?

"She looks like a teacher here," Shawna said.

"This lady's name was Ms. Brady," Kelley explained. "She used to teach English here. Rumor has it, she got pregnant by another teacher who was married. When she told him, he denied her and didn't want anything to do with her or the baby. She hung herself in her old classroom. One of her students found her the following day. It was in the hall Professor Briggs teaches in. And look at this, Shawna. Here's the guy who crashed his car by Dunn's creek. He used to go here, too."

Shawna's heart skipped a beat. "That," she said, "looks like Andrew."

"Who's Andrew?"

"He's a local guy. I see him walking all the time."

"Maybe this was his grandpa or something," Kelley said.

Shawna nodded, still eyeing the photo.

"Sad stuff," Kelley said, turning away from the trophy case. "Anyway, we should go. I don't want to be late to class, you know." She tapped an invisible watch on her wrist.

"Want to meet for lunch?" Shawna asked.

"Sure. And maybe I'll come hang out with you at your place tonight so I can see that hunka hunka Chandler." Kelley snorted mid-laughter.

"Sounds like a plan, but I work tonight."

"I know. I'll take up residence in a booth by the door and you can seat him with me when he comes to visit."

"I can do that." Shawna and Kelley turned toward their next classes, but before they could get far, Shawna said, "Do you know who those people over there are?"

Kelley shook her head and marched over to the group, where she stood and conversed for a short time. When she returned, Shawna asked, "Well?"

"Long story. I'll tell you tonight. We're going to be late, Miss Always-Punctual." She smiled, then said, "Shit. Don't look now."

Megan stepped in front of Kelley, opened her mouth to speak, almost did, but instead turned and walked away.

"What was that all about?" Shawna asked when Megan was out of earshot.

"That's my old roommate. She was too good to stay with me, and now she's dealing with a ghost in her new room." Shawna raised an eyebrow, to which Kelley responded, "I was going to warn her, but she decided to call me a freak. She's as bad as those sorority girls."

"I know you, Kelley," Shawna said, turning on her mothering voice. "You'll help her."

Kelley winked. "I'll give her some time to grovel a bit first."

"Bull. The minute she needs your help, you'll be there. That's just the kind of person you are."

"Probably, but don't tell her that."

Chapter 12

After her classes, Shawna was writing notes from her theology class outside the Robin's Nest before she had to start her shift when Chandler walked up. "What are you writing?" he asked.

"It's about Jacob's Stone," she said. "Well, the Stone of Jacob."

He nodded. "There was a battle when Babylon invaded the Holy Land. Jeremiah ended up with the stone and took it to Egypt with Myaletis, who was a Greek nobleman and mercenary. It was called the Pharaoh's Stone then."

"Wow," she said. "I didn't know you were into Biblical history."

He shrugged. "I'm into the history of that particular relic."

"So where did it go from there?"

"Scotland to Ireland by way of the Tribe of Dan or Towatha de Denan. It's called the Stone of Destiny now."

"You talk about it like it's someplace we can go see it now." She closed her notebook.

"It is. It's either in Scotland or Ireland. It's supposed to be, anyway. That's the last known public information I'm aware of regarding its whereabouts."

"I'd love to see it in person."

"Me, too."

"I'm actually a descendant of the tribe that brought it home." Chandler took a seat beside Shawna.

"You never told me that."

"And you haven't shared your ancestry with me, either. Nor your social security number. Strange."

She scoffed and nudged Chandler in the ribs. He grimaced, then continued. "It seems it doesn't matter now anyway. It was said the Jews were God's chosen people. Now, they say it's the Brit's. It's said, too, that the Stone of Destiny was in West Minster Abbey, and they returned it to Scotland recently. They called it the Coronation Stone, too. Kings and Queens would sit over it when they were sworn in to the throne."

"Why would they do that?"

"Good luck, I guess. It's said to have mystical powers. They called it the Stone of Scone, too. Jacob had a dream when he slept on it back then. He dreamed of a ladder to Heaven. Thus, the phrase, 'Jacob's ladder.' Another name for it is the Tanist Stone."

"Wow, Chand. You know a lot about it. We haven't gotten that far in class yet."

"I feel I know enough about it to write your report on it.' He laughed.

"Don't tell me anymore about it. I'll feel like I'm cheating. Plus, we're going to watch a movie about it in class this week. No more spoilers."

" She stood. "Kelley should be here soon. She was hoping to sit with you for a while."

"I won't be here long. I have to get to your place and let Beau out soon."

"Okay, but do you think you could talk to her? Politely listen? Maybe even feign interest? You'll sit with her, won't you?"

"I will, for you."

"You're the best," she said as she grabbed her books and bag to go into work, turned to Chandler and said, "Thank you."

He followed. "She's your friend, so I'm sure she's a nice girl."

"She is, Chand."

"Maybe she'll read my palm or cards or something."

"Stop it!" Inside the restaurant, she pointed to a near booth. "Sit." She grabbed three coffee cups, a pot of regular, 'leaded' coffee, as Kelley called it, and poured. She still had plenty of time before her shift started. The tiny bell hanging above the entrance dinged when Kelley walked in.

"Coffee?" Shawna asked when Kelley sat.

"Love some."

Shawna poured another cup and put the pot back on the burner. Chase, the busboy, was cleaning the section Shawna was scheduled to have that night. She waved lightly to him, to which he nodded and smiled.

Shawna felt a sudden twinge of guilt and wished she had had enough time to have visited Beau for a bit before coming to work. She worried that Beau was beginning to see Chandler as his Alpha, though she knew there was no one who would be better to care for him than Chandler if she couldn't be there all the time. For a moment, she considered quitting her job and letting her parents pay for everything the way they had offered. Then she'd have free time with Beau.

Seated beside Kelley, Shawna slapped her notebook onto the table.

"Are you doing homework?" Kelley asked.

"More studying?" Chandler said.

"No. It's my grocery list for tonight."

Up until then, Shawna had been tuning Kelley and Chandler's small talk out, but she realized then how strange Kelley was acting. She was staring at Chandler and wearing the goofiest smile. Shawna kicked Kelley under the table.

Kelley winced, but that didn't break her stare.

"Kelley!"

"What?"

"Are you, uh, staying the whole weekend?" Shawna said, eyes wide.

"Yep," she said, still staring.

"Do you want anything special from the store?"

"Yeah."

"And that is…? Forget it." Shawna stomped across the restaurant and came back with two menus to put between Kelley and the hunk of a man sitting in such close proximity to her, the dingbat.

"Thank you," Chandler said, relieved.

Shawna looked at him apologetically. He slapped both hands onto the table and stood. "I really need to go let Beau out," he said. Before Shawna could interject, he said, "But I'll be back. Kelley and I were just discussing her religion, and I'd like to hear more about it." He kissed Shawna on her cheek and left.

Kelley buried her nose in a book called *The Ancients and the Practical Use of Tarot, Crystals, and Other Divination Tools*. It was another Wiccan number. Another book was hanging out of Kelley's bag. This one was called *The Modern-Day Witch*.

Just as Shawna's mind swung back to her grocery list, the bell above the door tinkled again.

"Hey, Shawna."

"Hi, Paul! What brings you here?" She stood and hugged him lightly.

"The food smelled good, and I thought being here would give me a chance to see you again."

"Sit," she said, pointing across the table. "This is Kelley." While they exchanged pleasantries, Shawna poured him a glass of water. "You don't drink coffee, right?" she said when they'd finished.

"Can't stand it." He sipped the water and opened the menu Chandler had left behind. "Any specials today?"

"Good old burger and fries. How do you like your burger, sir?"

"Medium."

"Onions?"

"Love 'em."

"Grilled?"

"That's the best way."

"Pickles?"

"Please."

"Waffle fries?"

"Yep."

She sent the order back to the kitchen and refilled Kelley's coffee.

When she sat down, Paul said, "Aren't you working?"

"Only for you," she said. "My shift doesn't technically start until four. Besides, Lou and Dave are the only other people here." She nodded toward two regulars who sat hunched over the counter. Lou coughed. "Are you still living in town?"

He nodded. "Close to the pier. I've got a spot at the old campground. Are you still at that mansion in the country?"

"It's hardly a mansion, but yeah. And that's where I'll stay."

"Maybe I could swing by sometime." He sipped his water.

"That would be great."

As though he just realized Kelley was sitting at the table, he turned to her and asked, "Do you live near Shawna?"

"I live in a campus apartment," she said, turning a page in her book.

"That sounds cool."

"It's definitely not."

"Oh sorry."

A piercing *ding* rang from the kitchen, indicating that Paul's lunch was ready. Shawna tucked plenty of ketchup, mustard, salt, pepper, and napkins into the bag, then called, "Paul, do you want a can of pop with this?"

"No, thanks. I have some in my truck."

She wrote her phone number on the check stub and handed it to him. After he paid, told Kelley how nice it had been to meet her, and hugged Shawna again, he left.

Chandler returned just as the door had closed behind Paul. "Who was that?" he asked.

"An old friend I used to live by when we were kids. His name's Paul."

"An old boyfriend?"

"No, I thought he was cute when we were growing up, but I never told him."

Kelley chimed in with, "He'd have known if *I* liked him."

"Yeah, you're just a vixen, aren't you?" Shawna said.

"Maybe I am." Kelley said, but the truth was that she wasn't very outgoing at all. It was even worse when she was a kid. She used to be a scared little mouse. She was a different person back then. When she would talk to her Nana about her insecurities and all of the paranormal things happening to her when she was little, her Nana would say, "We all have to grow into our own skin sweetheart," and that comforted Kelley. Now, she was sure she had accomplished just that. She was a confident young woman and had accepted her spiritual awareness a long time ago. She used to hide under her covers at night when a spirit came to her for help, or she would yell for her Mother, who passed everything off as Kelley's imagination. Her Nana would visit frequently and console her because she had had the same experiences her whole life.

Nana once told her about a man who would visit her asking for his wife every night. Nana had lost her patience with him over the years, and one night "straightened him out" as she called it. In truth, she yelled at the poor guy and made him cross over. Nana told Kelley that her mother didn't have the sight and that she had no imagination to begin with, let alone an open mind and heart. "Don't worry when she doesn't believe you," Nana said. "I'm here to listen, and I'm only a phone call away." No matter what time it was, Kelley was to call her Nana if someone was bothering her. That made her feel so much better and got her through her childhood. She loves her Nana so much. She'd call her when she left here tonight.

Shawna said, "Down, Girl. Be nice, Kelley."

"I'll be very nice," she said with a big smile. She resumed her silly grin she wore when he sat across from her earlier.

"Are you guys ready to eat now?" Shawna asked.

"Mmmhmm," Kelley said.

Chandler saw the look Shawna was giving him, so he asked her what the special was. They decided on two of those with Dr. Peppers. Chandler, being a man of his word, started a conversation with Kelley, asking her about her classes at school. She told him that she was majoring in English and that she wanted to be a teacher, possibly a professor one day.

"Good for you," he said. "How does witchcraft fit in with teaching?"

"It actually fits in well with everything I do. I'm a very spiritual person," she said. "We Wiccans honor and observe both a Mother God and a Father God. Wicca is the religion I'm most drawn to. I'm a white witch. I worship Mother Nature, the Earth, the God, and the Goddess. We celebrate all Earth is and gives, and the cycles of the year. I'm into crystals. I don't actively practice witchcraft. Some do. I love candles and meditation. I celebrate the sun high in the sky, the first full moon, the trees letting their leaves, and the first snowfall. To me, it's an appreciation of all that Father God and Mother Goddess give us here on this plain. I'm into herbs and deep tissue massage, and I am totally opposed to medicine and doctors."

When she finally stopped talking, he said, "Well, at least you're a spiritual person."

"I am," she said. "I believe in and see spirits. I know we're not alone here. We never are. How do you feel about that?"

"I think that's cool"

"That's not what I meant."

Just then, Shawna sat down and asked what was with all the seriousness. "I was just explaining Wicca to Chandler," Kelley said.

"It's interesting, huh, Chand?" Shawna asked.

"Very," he answered.

"Order up!" The cook dinged a tiny bell in the kitchen window. Shawna brought Chandler and Kelley their drinks, then grabbed a handful of napkins and their plates. They ate and talked while Shawna waited other tables. She stopped by to ask how their food was on her way to the kitchen and asked if they wanted any dessert. She said, "I've got cherry pie, one of my favorites, as you guys know. There's banana cream pie, too."

"Mmm," Kelley said, her eyes glued to Chandler.

"We have apple pie, too," Shawna added. "All of them can come ala mode with the exception of the banana cream, of course. The best dessert here in my opinion is the chocolate cake with chocolate fudge icing. We have angel food cake with a raspberry glaze, too."

Kelley and Chandler both chose the angel food cake. "Go figure," Shawna said. "I'll be right back with them, and I'll bring a couple of ice-cold milks." They smiled. "What?" she asked. "I know what my friends like."

"She's awesome," Kelley said when Shawna had walked away.

"Yes, she is," Chandler said. He straightened in his seat. "You should be taking Theology with Shawna, Kelley."

"I'm not into monotheism. I don't think there's just one male God."

They kept on with small talk about school while Shawna bounced from table to table. Despite Shawna's insistence that she cover the tab, Chandler paid the bill at the register, and he and

Kelley left and went their separate ways. Shawna was annoyed that her friends had left a tip on the table, plus they didn't let her buy their dinners. She made a mental note to give the tip back when she saw them again.

After her shift, she found Kelley in the parking lot leaning against her car. That thing glowed in the dark!

"Who left the tip?" Shawna asked.

"Your boy toy. He wouldn't let me chip in, either. Not even on the tip."

"Sounds like him. So, are you guys going to see each other again?"

"Maybe in passing. That's about it, unfortunately. Some people are spooked by my whole belief system," Kelley said.

"Chandler doesn't judge, Kelley."

"Well, I could tell he didn't agree with what I was saying."

"Everyone has their own opinion. "Just look at it like that, Kel."

"Maybe. I'll follow you home." She got into her car, rolled down the window, and yelled, "I could just cast a love spell!"

Shawna laughed and said, "I'll meet you there. I'm going to the store first, remember?"

"Good. That'll give me a few minutes alone with Hottie."

"Whatever, crazy girl," Shawna smiled and shook her head. "See you there."

Chapter 13

Shawna headed out for the store. She wanted to get the stew cooked tonight. If it was done in time, she'd bring it to Andrew tonight. If not, she would deliver it tomorrow morning. She knew all the spices would be at home for her. Mom was on top of that stuff. She looked at the clock. It was already 8:15. She thought she would be lucky to stay up long enough to cook it, let alone deliver it that night. She resigned herself to the fact that at least she'd have it at home to cook it when she was able.

She grabbed the crystal from her pocket and looked at it, spinning it in her hand while the cashier rang up her groceries.

In the parking lot, a man began to walk toward her. Shawna felt uneasy and moved a parking row over, where a single woman was headed toward the store. She smiled at the woman as they were about to pass each other, ybut the stranger sidestepped directly in front of her.

Shawna stopped short of running face to face into the woman, whose eyes were milky white. Her breath! Oh, her breath! It smelled like the rotten hamburger that sat in the dumpster in the hot sun the week before garbage pick-up. Oh! Then, the woman tilted her head and a guttural noise rose from her stomach. She half moaned, half roared, "Dilatory!" with her blueish-black tongue hanging out of her crooked mouth and flopping around as if it were hanging by a vein, ready to fall right out. The woman seemed to be retching as she spoke.

Rattled beyond words, Shawna bolted. She had her keys out before she reached her car. She threw her bags in it and peeled out of the lot. Looking back in her rearview mirror, she saw the woman pointing at her car with the man beside her. They were joined by three others, all looking her way.

She made short work of the commute home and found Chandler waiting at the front door, Beau at his side. She ran into his arms crying.

He stiffened. "What's wrong?"

She told him what had happened between sobs.

"Maybe it was a homeless woman," he said. "Maybe she just needed help."

"A homeless woman? What about her purple tongue, Chandler?"

"It was dark in the parking lot, right? Maybe it just looked that way."

Shawna straightened her shoulders and sighed. "Well, she could have been nicer if all she needed was help. I would have gone back into that store and gotten her all kinds of food and shampoo and soap and a toothbrush with a gallon of mouthwash."

He chuckled lightly and brushed her hair behind her ear. "You're home now. No crazy ladies here."

He brought her inside, led her to the couch, and got her a glass of brandy. She sucked that down, got up, poured another one, and drank that in a few minutes. She hadn't told him what she thought she heard that horrible woman spew out, or the fact that she'd seen another woman in Professor Briggs's classroom write the same word on the chalkboard.

When Chandler went outside to get the groceries from Shawna's car, Beau jumped up on the couch next to her. She said, "I'm sorry, Baby." She nuzzled his neck. "I've been ignoring you."

Shawna's phone rang. It was Kelley.

"I was just going to call you," Shawna said instead of the usual "Hello." "I've got a lot I want to talk to you about. What time will you be here?"

Kelley told her that something had come up and she couldn't come tonight. She'd come tomorrow and stay the weekend.

"What's his name?" Shawna rolled her eyes.

"It's not a guy, Shay. If I were able, I'd be there tonight. Remember who's there with you. I'd take him over any guy I've ever met." She was quiet for a moment, then said, "My mom called. Nana is in the hospital."

"Oh, no! Nana Ruby? Is she going to be alright?"

Kelley looked over at her grandmother's spirit seated beside her and said, "I think so."

"Good. Are you okay?"

"I'm fine. I'll see you tomorrow."

Just after Shawna hung up, Chandler stood in the doorway and said, "I've got to get to work. Beau went out about an hour ago." She nodded and asked him to lock the doors on his way out. "Goodnight," he said, and she was alone.

***

Kelley's mother was speaking frantically into the phone. "Nana is right next to me," Kelley said. "She said to tell you she doesn't want to be on life support. She says to let her go."

Kelley's mother sniffled into the phone.

Kelley snorted.

"Is something funny?" her mother demanded.

"She says she doesn't want anybody else wiping her behind."

"But—"

"But nothing," Nana said. "You know how independent I've always been. Let me go."

"She says she's tired and old, and she wants to go to her reward," Kelley said. "I'll be right there."

Kelley dreaded hospitals, but she had no choice but to go there. When she arrived, two disembodied spirits were waving wildly in front of the receptionist's face, trying to get her attention. Kelley ignored them and asked for directions to Nana's room. The female spirit at the desk grew so frustrated that she knocked the receptionist's pens to the floor. She turned to Kelley. "You can see me, can't you?"

Kelley pretended to look through her.

"You can see me! You can! I saw you looking at me!"

Kelley nodded once.

Before the woman's spirit could continue, Nana appeared and rested a hand on Kelley's shoulder. "My granddaughter can see both of you," Nana said. "But she can't help you until she speaks with my daughter. You can follow us, but you'll have to wait your turn. Do you understand, young lady?"

The woman opened her mouth to speak, but Nana shushed her. She said, "Nod if you understand."

The woman nodded, and the man stood mute but followed along politely. Kelley, with three invisible spirits in tow, made her way to Nana's room, where her mother was clutching Nana's hand and crying silently.

"Nana's with me, Mom," Kelley said.

Her mother turned around expecting to see Nana standing beside Kelley, but she could see nothing. She spoke, nonetheless, staring off at something over Nana's shoulder. Nana cracked up laughing, sending Kelley into a fit of giggles. The man and woman's spirits were standing in the doorway and began to laugh too.

"Why would you laugh at a time like this?" Kelley's mother demanded.

"Sorry, Mom. It's Nana's fault." She turned to Nana and said, "Nana! Stop it!"

Nana moved to her daughter's side.

"She's on your right, Mom."

Kelley's mother looked to her right and said, "Mother, I don't want to lose you."

"Tell her she won't," Nana said. "We'll be together soon. Sooner than she thinks."

"Why would you say something like that, Nana?"

"Time goes by quickly. Before she knows it, she'll be my age, and she'll want you to pull the plug on her, too!"

Kelley stifled another laugh and said, "Nana says that you won't be losing her. She'll always be with you, in your heart, waiting for you on the Other Side."

"What if she's wrong? And, I know my own mother. I'm sure she had more to say than that."

Kelley ignored the last bit.

"As ornery as she is, she could have twenty more years." Kelley's mother tried to face Nana again. "Just give it a couple more weeks, please—no more than a month. You'll wake up and I'll tell you I told you so."

Kelley's Nana conceded, and she sat next to her daughter to watch her watching herself. She thanked Kelley for coming up and trying to reason with her mom. She said, "She's wrong, you know."

"Well, let her have this, Nana. It's not hurting you to stick around for a few more weeks. Then you can go home."

Kelley's mom, overhearing Kelley's part of the conversation, said, "Thank you!"

Kelley helped the other spirits and left the woman with the same resolution she had her Nana. The man had had brain surgery and wasn't waking up from it. He had two little boys sitting next to his bed crying in their mom's lap. She was crying too. Kelley gave them his message, and the man stuck around for them until the wife could get ahold of his family out of town and she could inform them that he was going to donate his organs. Soon he would be going home to the Other Side. He thanked Kelley for delivering his messages.

Done with them, Kelley called Shawna and told her about her Nana's antics. Shawna wasn't surprised. She said how sorry she was for Kelley's family, though. "Kiss Nana for me," she said. "See you soon."

On her way home from the hospital, the spirit of a man showed up in the front seat of Kelley's car and startled her. She said, "You know, if I wasn't used to this, I could have an accid—

The car veered off the road and into a shallow ditch.

Kelley woke up to a burning sensation in her nose and throat. They had used smelling salts to bring her back to consciousness. She was taken for an M. R. I. as soon as she got to the E.R., then x-rays after that. She wasn't happy at all about any of this. It was a different hospital than the one her Nana was in. On the way to the tests, she saw many spirits. Some followed her to her tests. She closed her eyes but couldn't shut out their voices or her desire to help them.

The doctors didn't find anything immediately life threatening, but she was admitted for a concussion and because they were hoping to treat her other condition. Doctors and spirits were hovering over her in the hospital bed. One was speaking of M.R.I.s and she heard the 'C' word. That was all she needed to hear. She got up and got dressed in a huff. She grabbed her phone and called Shawna. She got her voicemail.

A nurse entered Kelley's room and asked her why she was up and about.

"You can keep your poison!" Kelley said. "I'm leaving. My friend is coming to get me."

Kelley was sure she knew where the tow company had taken her car. There was only one towing service in town. A guy she went to school with, Jake Robertson, owned the business. Despite the nurses' objections, Kelley got a ride with Jake, who dropped her off at her apartment. She thanked him, and he went on his way.

Chapter 14

Shawna pulled the crystal out of her pocket, set it on the table by her drink, polished off her brandy, and got up to get cleaned up for bed. *Groceries,* she thought. She had to put them up before she went upstairs. As she began stacking cans in the cabinet, she caught a glimpse of something out of the corner of her eye. She thought she saw the little neighbor girl outside her patio door and did a double take. It was her! Shawna went to the door and opened it, and there she stood in the same clothes she always wore.

"It's you!" the girl said.

"Well yeah, it's me. I'm the one whose yard you're in, and I'm the one who almost hit you backing out of my driveway more than once. You're always by yourself. Why? And at all hours of the night. Where are your parents?"

"I don't know."

"Are you hungry?"

She shook her head.

"Are you hurt?"

"I don't think so."

"Do you want to come in and call home?"

She shook her head again.

"What's your name?"

"Tracey."

"Tracey what?"

"Paxton."

Shawna raised her eyebrows. Could she be related to the Paxton's Shawna knew of? A Paxton wouldn't be out running around unattended. She shrugged it off and assumed the girl belonged to another family of Paxton's. "You should probably get home now. Your parents must be worried about you."

The girl nodded but stood in her place.

Then, *Boom!*

Boom!

Boom!

The house vibrated with each barrage. Shawna jumped. The girl stood stock still. Wide eyed, Shawna stared at the basement door from where she stood but composed herself before turning back to the girl. She didn't want to frighten her. "Well, run along then."

The girl slumped and walked away. Shawna went inside, walked to the basement door, and opened it. Beau ran up to her and got between her and the stairwell. She moved him aside and said, "We've got to go see what that was, buddy." Beau let out a low growl. Shawna heard scratching and bangs coming from down there. She turned on the basement light, got halfway down the stairs, and the light turned off. It came back on again and went off and on like someone was standing there flipping the switch, flicking it on, off, on, off.

Heart thudding, Shawna ran up the steps and called Beau to come with her. She slammed the door and locked it.

As tempting as bed was, Shawna knew she had to shower. She had to get that funk off of her that came from that woman who she only stood close to. She could imagine how she'd stink if she was touched by her.

After her shower, she called Kelley while she waited for Chandler to get home. She got her voicemail and just hung up. She decided to make that stew after all even though whatever had made that noise was on the other side of the door that was in her kitchen. She started it, hoping to distract Beau and herself with the smells of it while waiting for Chandler to get home. She couldn't get that door off of her mind, so she put the stew on simmer and went into the living room with Beau.

She sat on the couch covered up with Beau under a blanket watching T.V. Candles Kelley had given her were lit around the room. Watching the clock for Chandler to get back, Beau by her side, she tried to relax but couldn't stop her imagination from getting the best of her. Every little noise, any shadow, had her on the edge of her seat. She grabbed her cell and dialed Kelley again.

"Hey, babe. What's up?"

"I really wish you would've stayed here tonight. There are some noises coming from my basement, and the lights are going on and off. It's really freaking me out."

"Lock that door!"

"Way ahead of you. It's not helping my nerves, though."

"I'm on my way."

"Thanks, Kel. I made that stew, so maybe we can all take it to Andrew tonight. It'll give us a good reason to get out of here."

"Sure. I'm finishing up packing now. I'll have to sneak out of here, but I'll be there soon."

Chapter 15

Still dressed in her pajamas, Shawna waited with Beau on the front porch for Kelley to arrive. About twenty minutes later, Kelley showed up. Shawna noticed the big dent on her car and a bandage on Kelley's forehead.

Shawna said, "I'm sorry. You should have told me you got hurt. I wouldn't have asked you to come."

"Oh," Kelley said, ripping off the bandage. "I forgot this was here. I would have taken it off a long time ago."

"What happened?"

"Fender bender."

"Did someone hit you? Are you alright?"

"I'm fine. You should see the other guy." She laughed and snorted. "I was bothered when I was driving. Don't worry so much. I'm here, so I'm okay." She grabbed all of her "goodies" out of the car. Shawna couldn't believe all the things Kelley had in her arms. She looked as if she were holding half of her wardrobe.

"Don't judge," Kelley said. Shawna smiled and grabbed some of the clothes that fell out of a bag. There was a flannel shirt, leggings, a tennis shoe. "What's this? Lingerie?" Shawna asked. "What on earth do you need—Oh!" she said. She had a slinky, see-through number between her forefinger and her thumb, and the crotchless panties fell out from the set. If you could call that teensy piece of material panties! Shawna picked them up as if she were picking up a dead mouse, and with as much chagrin. Kelley rolled her eyes, balled up the panties, and said, "Moving on! This stuff's not getting any lighter."

Shawna chuckled.

"Well, you never know if he'll see me in my pajamas when he walks past your room."

"Pajamas? I'm not hanging around you while you're wearing *that*. And you're definitely not sleeping in *my* bed wearing it either!"

"Who said I was planning to end the night in your room, anyway?"

Shawna sighed heavily. "Just wear a shirt over it and some shorts." She piled the lingerie on top of Kelley's load, which towered in front of her face. Shawna laughed. Peering through the lingerie, looking at Shawna, Kelley said, "Very funny."

"I thought it was."

After Kelley got settled in, the girls made some popcorn and sandwiches. Shawna checked the stew. It was done. They put their sandwiches up for later. Shawna asked Kelley to get some blankets, pillows, and Shawna's tent and backpacks out of the linen and hallway closets. They packed it all in the car and went back in for the stew while Beau waited in the car for them.

The trio drove to Dunn's Creek, saw people gathered there, parked by the bridge, and asked a guy what the attraction was. He told them that there was a body down there, pointing to where Shawna assumed Andrew was living. Shawna started to run down there. Kelley yelled for her to stop. She said, "When you find out it's not him, you're going to wish we'd brought all this stuff down there for him with you now!"

"How do you know it's not him?"

Kelley pointed to a stretcher being carried by paramedics with a shock of long blond hair hanging off of it and a woman's arm that had fallen out from beneath a white sheet. Shawna was relieved that it wasn't Andrew, but she still felt bad for the woman and her family.

The girls hiked down the hill at one end of the bridge. They stepped over craggy rocks to get to the spot underneath the bridge where she thought they'd find Andrew. They both wore the backpacks to carry everything except the stew. Shawna left that in the crockpot she had transferred it to after she browned the meat on the stove, so that had to be carried by hand. Kelley stayed back to give them the privacy she thought was needed to not embarrass the guy. Beau, who had beaten the girls down to the spot under the bridge, ran up to Andrew as if he knew him already.

Shawna called for Andrew. After three times calling for him without a response, she was ready to leave. Just as she was turning away, Andrew stepped out from underneath the bridge with a woman. Beau popped out from under there, tail wagging.

"Andrew, is that you?"

"Yes."

"I brought you some food. I had a lot of leftovers." She set the Crockpot down, dropped her backpack, and took Kelley's bag. "Here's a tent, some pillows, and blankets, too, in case you know anyone who can use them."

"It's you," he said, ignoring the bag.

"What?"

"Thank you," he said.

She frowned a moment and continued. "There are rolls and butter and spoons in there. Everything you need for a nice meal tonight. I hope you know someone who will share it with you."

She pulled bottles of water out of one of the backpacks and set them at the water's edge. "I'll see you around."

He nodded, and the girls left for Shawna's house. Something caught Shawna's eye as they were driving off. She said, "Look! That can't be him all the way up here on the bridge! How'd he beat us up here?"

Kelley looked and said, "If it is him, he should be sitting in a tent cozying up to a bowl of hot stew, not climbing rocks."

"I know! And, I made it especially for him!"

"His loss," Kelley said, and they drove away.

When they got back to the house, Kelley went into the living room and laid out the goodies she brought. Shawna walked toward that room after she got their sandwiches from the kitchen, stopped short in front of the basement door, and double-checked the lock. Kelley heard the rattle of the knob from where she was and came to see what was going on. She said, "Let's go see if you have a ghosty." She moaned exaggeratedly and wiggled her fingers in front of Shawna's face.

"Not funny, Kel."

"Sorry, but we do need to put your fears to rest. It's probably just your furnace, a broken water pipe, an electrical switch issue, something like that. Or a ghost!"

Shawna sighed. "Fine. I'll go down there and look since you're here."

Shawna opened the door, flipped on the switch, and stood there waiting for it to go back off, but it didn't. Beau pushed his way between the two of them and went ahead of them down the stairs. They checked every room one by one. The last one they came to had a door made of lead.

"That's weird. Are you hiding a safe full of riches down here, or what?" Kelley asked.

"I don't even know what's back there, honestly. I haven't spent much time down here since we moved in." She reached for the door, but it was locked.

"I bet the noise is coming from in there." Kelley shoved the door, but it wouldn't budge.

83

"I doubt a burglar's going to break in and lock himself in a dusty room. Let's just go back upstairs."

As they turned to leave, Beau started growling at the door. His ears were pinned back, and the hair on his back stood upright.

"See?" Kelley pushed on the door again. "There's something in there that he doesn't like."

Shawna didn't come any closer to the door. "Come on, Beau," she said. "Let's go upstairs." Beau barked a few times but reluctantly followed the girls upstairs. Shawna locked the door from the kitchen to the basement again just in case. She had a bad feeling about the basement. Kelley did too, but she didn't tell Shawna for fear of making her even more scared than she already was.

They grabbed some more food from the kitchen, grabbed a bottle of wine and some glasses, and sat down on the couch. Shawna saw that Kelley had laid everything out that she had brought with her. "A Ouija board?" she asked.

Kelley shrugged. "I thought we'd—

"No! Not a chance. I've heard bad things about those." This was her home, her safe haven, and nothing was getting stirred up around here because of that stupid game.

"It depends on your intent whether anything bad will come of using it, Shawna. Relax."

"I don't care."

"I'm not a dark person, Shay. You know that."

"I'm not playing with that thing. I don't even want it in my house. How could you bring that here?"

"Would you relax, Shawna? I've been noticing a change in you lately, like you're not yourself. I was going to try to see what's wrong and help you, but I needed my Guide's help."

"It's true that there are a lot of things bothering me lately, but right now, that board is bothering me more than anything." She took a deep breath. "Would you please get that thing out of my house?"

"Ugh, just give me a second. Don't get your panties in a bunch."

"At least I'm wearing some."

Kelley got up to take the board to the car and said, "F.Y.I., I'm wearing a cute pair of boy shorts right now."

"Good! Leave them on all night. And bring those crotchless things back out to your car with you, too."

"Not a chance. I'll take the board out, but I have plans for those babies."

"Gross."

Chapter 16

"Who's that little girl out front?" Kelley asked when she came inside.

"If I had to guess, I'd say it's Tracey Paxton. That kid never goes home," Shawna said.

"Maybe it's because she doesn't have one anymore. She's the one you've almost hit like three times backing out, right?"

Shawna nodded slowly.

"And is she always in that green checkered jumper?"

She nodded again. "But what does that—

"Shay. You see her all the time. Think about it."

Shawna's eyes widened. "No."

"Yes."

Shawna rubbed her chin. "That's not the only thing that's been happening to me lately." She went on to tell her about the people in the parking lot and how she could hardly get the smell of that woman out of her hair after repeated washings. She felt like she could still taste that smell. She told her about the woman in Professor Briggs' classroom that day, too.

"And Professor Briggs didn't see her?" Kelley asked.

"No. Either she fell through a trapdoor or—

"She was a ghost! Congratulations, Shay. You see them too!"

"Why now?"

"Some people's sixth sense is finer tuned than others."

"I don't know about all that."

"You lived in a haunted house, Shawna, and you saw them then."

"I know, but I was very small then. We're all capable of seeing things when we're young, but we grow out of that."

"That's because young people are the most recent arrivals from the Other Side. As we get older, we're told that we're imagining things and seeing things. Parents try to downplay everything they're told. I think it's more out of their own fear than anything." Kelley tucked her hair behind her ear. "It's easy for them to dismiss what the kids tell them as imagination. People sort of get programmed to not believe anything they don't see for themselves."

"I'm seeing things regularly now."

"Because you have that crystal now. I'm sure that has a lot to do with it."

"You can't say they're all spirits or ghosts though, Kelley. They could just be strange people. I can't tell the difference."

"I can. The auras around people who have passed but not crossed are different than yours and mine. Spirits are harder to see than ghosts. A ghost's aura is a mucky gray, almost like a thick, muddy fog."

"That's what those people at school had around them, the ones we thought were there for a play."

They were ghosts?"

Kelley nodded excitedly. "I'd bet a date with Hottie on it."

"I wonder what they wanted."

"I don't know, but I want to find out. They wouldn't talk to me. I don't understand why. By the way, your aura's purple." She winked and said, "Let's see that crystal again." Shawna pulled it from her pocket. Kelley rolled it in her fingers. "Selenite's very powerful," she said. "It's said to be able to open up a person to the Other Side and to spirits and your ghosties."

Shawna straightened and rolled her eyes. "Like I need that."

"I'll take it from you if you don't want it."

"No, I love the stone. I just don't need the spooks that come along with it."

"Well, it's not guaranteed that you'll have issues, but when you're open to it, it stands to reason that you might. Like, say if I owned it, my social calendar would be filled up spiritually." She dug into her bag and withdrew a stack of long cards. "Let's read your cards now. Are you relaxed?"

"Not really."

"I'm thinking we need a margarita. How about it?"

Shawna reached into the cooler next to the couch and said, "Here's your margarita."

Kelley eyed the beer can in her hand and raised an eyebrow at Shawna.

"I don't have the stuff to make margaritas." She grabbed the bottle of wine she had taken from her dad's personal collection earlier. She stood and presented the bottle to Kelley like she was the server in a restaurant. "Madam." She bowed. "A Nineteen-thirty-four Bordeaux, a Haute-Brion."

Kelley giggled. "As long as it tastes good and we get a buzz from it, that's fine with me."

Shawna opened the bottle and set it aside with their empty glasses.

"What are you doing? Make with the special grape juice already."

"We have to let it breathe a while."

"Hmph." She slapped her thighs. "I'll just sage the house then." Over the next fifteen minutes, Kelley addressed every closet, every corner, every nook and cranny in every room, carrying a burning bundle of sage and pushing its smoke around the house. The only area she missed was the locked room in the basement. The smell wafted up around her, but she insisted on doing it to herself and Shawna again prior to the reading of the cards.

Shawna opened up the front screen door, propped it open, and went to the kitchen and opened the patio door. "You know,"

Kelley said, "since I've done all of this, it would be safe to use the board now. I can just sage that outside."

"I don't know," Shawna said. "Maybe."

"Good. We'll set it all up on the table after you pour me some of that wine." Shawna poured them each a glass. "That's good." Kelley licked her lips.

"Told you so. It's one of Daddy's special reserve."

"That's too good to put away and not drink."

"The more it sits, the better it gets."

"He won't be mad we're having it, will he?"

Shawna shook her head. "He told me I could have any of them I wanted."

"Sounds like a plan. We might just have to open up another one of these." Kelley handed her glass to Shawna. "Hold this." She went outside and stooped to pull the board from her car. Just as she stood, she saw the little neighbor girl watching her. "Hey there," Kelley said to her. "You must be Tracey."

The girl nodded.

"Why aren't you home?"

Tracey pointed to Shawna's house and said, "I can't go."

Kelley's eyes widened in sudden understanding. She sucked in a deep breath and said, "I think you'll be able to go home soon."

The girl smiled and tears welled in her eyes before she disappeared.

Kelley saged the board, the planchette, and even the box it came in while she sat on the grass. After, she went inside with it, leaving the door unlocked and open, and the screen door ajar, just as it had been when she went out. She set the board on the coffee table in front of the couch and saged the cards individually. Then she handed them to Shawna and said, "Okay. Relax and breathe deeply, open your heart and mind, and shuffle them. I got my energy all over them, and I've cleansed them. There are just over seventy cards here, so if you can't shuffle them the traditional way, do it on the table. Then, cut the cards."

Chapter 17

"I'm thinking the Celtic cross for you," Kelley said, eyeing the cards in Shawna's hands.

"The what?"

"It's a method of reading cards. It has to do with the number of cards that a person reading has you pick and the way they're laid out. There's a simple three card layout, too, called the horseshoe spread. That's pretty much the most popular layout, but for my own reasons, I'm drawn to the Celtic cross for you."

"Why?"

"Call it intuition. My sixth sense. You need a problem solved. You have questions." She took the cards from Shawna and laid one in front of her: The Queen of Wands.

"Wait. What does that mean?'

"Just what it looks like, really. The black cat represents a darker side to the Queen."

"Cat? What cat?"

"See the cat at the queen's feet?"

"Oh. What do the lions mean?"

"Technically, it means you've been called upon to be a loving master of integrity. Don't worry about the lions, and the card doesn't mean you're royalty either. Let me lay them all out, and put the pieces together for you."

Shawna nodded.

"Let's just say this card represents you well. It means you put others before yourself. It says you are you, Shay, but we'll see what all of them together mean." Kelley drew another card: Queen of Cups. "More of the nurturing stuff that describes you," she said, "but more for older women, really." She drew a third card: Death.

"What is that?" Shawna's heart leapt in her throat.

"It means resistance to change. That's all." Kelley drew another card and said, "Card number four is the Ace of Pentacles, which represents the beginning of something new. Number five: the Lovers. Is it him?"

"No! We're friends. I told you that."

"Okay, okay. The Lovers card means you shouldn't put your mental expectations or fantasies before your physical ones with this mystery dude."

They needed more room with the board, crystals, and bundles of sage and sweetgrass spread out all over, so Kelley reached for the board. As she moved it, the planchette started sliding to the floor. Shawna and Kelley reached for it together, but Shawna reached it first, surprising herself. She placed it on the board and wiped her hand on her pants, as though washing away any risk of encountering evil.

The planchette began to spin, swirling and swirling until it landed on the 'D,' then the 'I' and the 'L.'

A rustling sound behind them drew their attention from the planchette. Chandler stood in the doorway, mouth agape. He stomped forward and slammed the planchette with his fist. "You know better than this, Shawna! You know not to bring this into your house." He huffed off up the stairs.

"It was spelling that word again," Shawna said, her voice low.

"Judging by the way he seems to be upset by my bringing that here, I'm guessing it was telling me I should have brought my D-I-L-D-O." She chuckled.

"This is serious, Kelley."

"Yeah, and so is finishing a reading of the cards, so let's finish up."

"Get rid of that board first."

"Fine. I'll take it outside."

When they were finished, Shawna got a basic, generic reading that said she had something important to do, she was very spiritual and responsible, and she was going to have a new love interest, which she lacked at the moment. She doubted she ever would, but three out of four wasn't bad as far as she was concerned. Letting a new guy in was a negative; however, Paul was coming over soon. She liked him a lot, and she might be ready to let him in just a little bit. It had been a long time since she had any attention in that arena.

"Kelley, I'm worried now about that stupid board."

"Don't be. If there's anything to it, it's only positive after all the cleansing I've done here."

"Speaking of that, can you get the rest of your stuff off of the table so I can clean it?"

"Let me sage us again first."

"If you think it's necessary."

"I think I should."

"Do it then!"

"Sheesh, Shawna, you're testy!"

"Well, now I've got Chandler upset with me."

"It's your house, and he's a guest here. He's not your father."

"He's concerned for my well-being."

"I'm your best friend. I wouldn't do anything to hurt you."

"I know, Kel. I just wish we wouldn't have brought that board in here."

"It's gone now, so let's finish that bottle of wine and try to relax," Kelley said.

"Alright." She tossed the remote to Kelley and said, "I'll be right back." Kelley flipped through the channels and found a paranormal show with one of her favorite lady psychics. Noise sounded from the basement, but it was louder than ever before. The booms, scratching, and rattles all came in sets of three. Kelley's hairs stood on end as she turned toward the basement door. She knew what three noises in a row meant. It was a mocking of the Holy Trinity.

Suddenly, Shawna and Chandler came bounding down the stairs with Beau in the lead. Beau barked ferociously at the basement door, and when Chandler opened it, Beau bolted down the steps and stood barking and growling in front of the mystery room. The lead door rattled with every bang and knock coming from inside.

Chandler tried the door. "Do you have a key?"

"No, but I have John coming tomorrow," Shawna said. "He's the handyman. He should have keys to everything. Otis, our groundskeeper, will be here too."

He nodded. "I don't leave until tomorrow night, so I'll be here when he opens it. There's nothing we can do now."

"I'm wondering how long you've been listening to that before you called me," Kelley called from the top of the stairs.

"It's been a while, but it's never been this loud."

Chapter 18

"We need to talk, Shawna," Chandler said.

Shawna's heart leapt into her throat. "Are you still mad about—

"I have to go away for a while."

"What?"

"But I don't think it will be for more than a week, if that long. I'll be back as soon as I can."

"Do you have to go right away? Can't it wait? Where are you going?"

He shook his head. "I'm afraid it can't, but maybe Kelley can stay with you while I'm gone."

Kelley nodded.

"I wish you didn't have to leave," Shawna said.

"Me too," Kelley added.

"I do. It's a favor for a relative."

Shawna stared at her feet, unsure of what to say next. "When are you leaving?"

"I'm leaving on the red eye tomorrow night." He rested a gentle hand on her shoulder. "If I didn't have to, I wouldn't go, but I'm keeping a promise I made a long time ago."

"I thought you meant you were leaving for work tomorrow night."

"I know you did."

Shawna frowned. "I'll see you before you leave, though, right?"

"You will."

"We can have breakfast together."

"All of us," Kelley said. Chandler ignored her.

The noises sounding from downstairs were now dull thuds.

"I really wish that noise would stop," Shawna said. "I don't know if I'm going to be able to sleep."

"You're safe," Chandler said. "I won't let anything happen to you."

"Besides," Kelley said, "that door isn't opening. Whatever's in there is staying until we get that key."

Shawna sighed and turned to Kelley. "Are you ready to head upstairs for the night.?"

She nodded.

Chandler made his way to his room, and Shawna, Kelley, and Beau headed for Shawna's bedroom.

"I guess I don't need these anymore," Kelley said, flinging her lingerie across the room like a slingshot.

She turned the light off and flopped onto the bed beside Shawna. Beau lay between them.

"Kel?" Shawna asked.

"Hm?"

"Is my home still clean?"

"What?"

"Is it still safe here now since that board's been in my house?"

"Honestly, Shay, I don't know." She ran her fingers through her hair and stared up at the ceiling. "Like I said before, everything I do, I do with love and respect, so it was nothing I did. But I can't understand why the planchette was moving on its own."

"Well, we were both touching the board in the beginning."

"Yeah, I think that was the catalyst, but it's just—I've never seen that before. We didn't ask any questions to attempt any communication whatsoever. It just makes my spidey senses start tingling. What I *do* know, though," she said, propping herself up on one elbow, "is that you and Beau shouldn't stay here alone."

Shawna gently massaged Beau's silky ear between her thumb and index finger. "He's going to miss Chandler. But he'll get used to it. It's only a week or so. I don't want him here by himself, though, when you and I are both busy."

"Tell your boss you need a week off, then."

"We can't change our schedules with such short notice. And then there are our classes, too." She straightened, eyes wide with an idea. "I'll just talk to Jess and see if Beau can hang out with him and Gussy at their place while we're gone. I should have thought of that sooner."

Kelley smiled. "Feel better?"

"Emotionally, yes. Physically, not so much. You guys are hogging the bed."

"It's not me! I'm on the edge."

Shawna reached over and felt her buddy's face. His was facing hers, and she put her arm around him and kissed his cheek and said, "'Night, my love." He gave her a flick of a kiss on her nose. Satisfied with that, she drifted off to sleep, but she had a horrible dream. It was one of two she'd been having again and again lately. In this one, she felt like the pied piper with people following her again in a cemetery until a wraith-like figure popped up from the ground in front of her and scared the people off.

Then, her dream changed to memories of the house she lived in prior to this one until she woke up the next morning. Kelley tossed and turned as much as she could move, as close to the edge as she was. She sat up and saw Beau sleeping soundly with his head on Shawna's pillow. No wonder! She had been given the business end of the dog! On cue, he stretched and farted. "Thanks a lot, dog!" She waved a hand in front of her nose and got up griping about what the hell he had eaten yesterday on her way into the ensuite to get a breath of fresh air and a drink of water when she saw something out of her peripheral vision in the hallway.

A smell worse than the dog's gas wafted in from the hallway, burning her nose and throat. Beau grunted and lifted his head accusatorily toward Kelley.

"It wasn't me!" she said.

Both Beau and Kelley turned to Shawna then, who was still sound asleep on her side.

"No, it wasn't your princess either!"

Beau grunted again, rolled onto his back, and threw his front and back leg over Shawna.

The smell having subsided, Kelley walked quietly into the hallway, listening to muffled voices coming from Chandler's room. She swore Chandler was talking to someone. Did he have a different woman in there? She thought. She pressed her ear to the door just as it whipped open.

"Is the T.V. too loud?" he asked, shoulders straight.

She stepped back and smiled faintly. "I was just getting a drink, and I thought I heard something."

"I'll keep it down." He closed the door in her face.

She tousled her hair, wishing she had brushed it or done an eyebooger check before spying on Chandler. She held her hand in front of her face and breathed heavily into it before sniffing her palm and wincing. "Ugh." She looked down at her very modest nightgown and shook her head. It wasn't what she'd had in mind for running into him in the middle of the night. "Shit," she whispered. She started back toward Shawna's room but stopped in her tracks. Her sixth sense was pulling her toward the stair landing.

Chapter 19

From the top of the stairs, Kelly peered down and saw that little neighbor girl seated on the couch in the living room. She wasn't alone; several others gathered around her. More stood in the hallway.

As quietly as she could, Kelley moved down the stairs.

More people were gathered in the kitchen. Some had even taken the liberty of browsing the pantry contents. They mingled and chatted as though they were all guests at some secret party Kelley hadn't been invited to. A middle-aged man moved through the group carrying a tray of champagne-filled glasses, nearly bumping into Kelley. She raised an eyebrow and reached for a glass, but her fingers passed through the glass's stem. She tapped the man on the shoulder, but her hand passed through him too.

"Freaky dream," she said to herself, shaking her head lightly. She ran a hand along her scalp, staring at her feet as she plodded back up the stairs and to Shawna's bedroom. Kelley fell back to sleep until her alarm sounded four hours later.

Shawna hit the snooze button and stood, immediately thinking of Chandler's imminent departure. She showered more quickly than she normally would and left Kelley snoring in the bed beside Beau. Beau opened his eyes as Shawna was leaving, squeaked out another fart for good measure, and hopped out of bed. Kelley choked on the smell in her sleep and rolled over.

Beau found Shawna downstairs in the kitchen. She let him outside and started a pan full of sausage links. As the sausage began sizzling, she sliced various fruits and left a medley in a bowl on the table, hoping that the smell of breakfast would be enough to wake the others.

As though on cue, Kelley padded down the stairs, her hair mussed, eyes at half-mast.

"You cook like this every morning?" she asked, stretching and scratching the top of her head. "I'm glad I'm staying here for a while."

"Don't get used to it," Shawna said, waving a spatula at Kelley. "I just wanted Chandler to have a good breakfast before he left."

Kelley grabbed a slide of banana from the bowl, poured a cup of coffee, and sat back down. "You really love him," she said.

"I do love him. I love him the same way I love you. You're my best friends."

"Yeah. Okay," Kelley said through a mouthful of banana. She rolled her eyes.

Steady footsteps sounded from the stairs. Kelley leapt from the table and checked her reflection in the side of the toaster. She drug her fingertips along her lower eyelids to wipe away any remnants of yesterday's smudged makeup and flattened her hair.

She hopped back into her chair and leaned back, popping a bite of raspberry Danish in her mouth. She glanced down at her gown and unbuttoned the top two buttons.

Shawna grunted and rolled her eyes.

Then there he was, shirt tucked in, shoes shining, hair slicked back. He smelled amazing. He walked into the kitchen and hugged Shawna.

"You didn't have to do all of this," he said.

From over his shoulder, Shawna saw Kelley mouth, "Damn!" before fanning herself exaggeratedly.

Kelley smiled at him as he turned around. Bits of Danish clung to her teeth.

"Good morning, Kelley," he said politely.

She flushed.

Beau gave a light bark from outside the door. When Shawna let him inside, he seemed to bathe himself in the wonderful scents circling about the kitchen. He lapped at his bowl of water and splattered droplets across the floor.

"I've got everything packed. I can't give you a number for where I'll be yet, but you have my cell number."

"How long before you leave?" Shawna asked.

"I'll be here until you two go to sleep tonight."

Kelley smiled to herself, thinking of how badly she would like to give him a sendoff he wouldn't soon forget.

"I'm sorry about the T.V. disturbing you last night," he said to Kelley.

She nearly choked on another bite of Danish. "That was real?" she said to herself, realizing too late that she had said it loudly enough for the others to hear.

"Did you think you were dreaming?" Chandler asked.

She nodded and smiled. "Guess I wasn't." She bit her lip and continued, "It seemed like there were more people here last night than just us three."

Chandler raised an eyebrow but said nothing. He poured a cup of coffee.

"I'll be going overseas," he said.

"This favor must be very important, then," she said.

"Of the utmost importance," he said. "I made a promise, and I keep my promises. You know that." He sat across from Kelley. "I don't expect this trip to last just a few days. Are you able to stay for at least a week, Kelley?"

"Hell, if there's breakfast like this every day, you'll be lucky to get rid of me by the time you get back."

He nodded.

"What time's the guy with the keys coming?" Kelley asked.

"He should be here soon," Shawna said.

Chandler stood and reached across the table for the newspaper, sending a waft of his scent toward Kelley. She inhaled deeply and nearly shuddered. He smelled like chocolate cake.

"Excuse my reach," he said.

"No problem." She had hoped he'd just sit where the paper had been, closer to her.

"Over easy, or scrambled?" Shawna asked, spatula still in hand. "Kelley?"

"Huh?"

"How do you want your eggs? Over easy or not?"

"That's fine. Thanks."

"Chand? How about yours?"

"However you want to make them will be fine," he said, nose in the newspaper.

She added three more eggs to the pan for him, then busied herself with the toast, flipped the eggs, and asked Kelley to grab the plates from the cupboard. When Kelley didn't stand up soon enough, Shawna got them herself.

"Kelley? You in there?"

"Hm?" She had been examining Chandler's fingertips from the back side of the newspaper. He was so well-manicured, yet still so…manly.

"Could you pour some milk and put more toast in, please?"

"Sure." Kelley stood and helped arrange the rest of their breakfast. She poured three glasses of milk and set them on the table, just as Shawna was bringing heaping plates. "Hash browns too? Shay, you've outdone yourself."

Chandler folded his newspaper and set it aside. "She always makes breakfast like this at least once a weekend." He winked at Shawna and added, "Thank you."

Conversation died down as the three enjoyed their meals, filling the kitchen with the sound of forks clinking lightly on ceramic plates. Then, the sounds began again.

Boom. Boom. Boom.

Bam, bang, Clink, Crash,

A roar, scratches and crashes sounded from the basement. Shawna exclaimed. "What the?"

"Where's Beau?" Chandler asked.

"Right here." Shawna pointed under the table, where Beau sat, ignoring the sound for the sake of possibly catching a piece of crust or a bite of sausage.

Boom! Boom! Boom!

Scratch! Scratch! Scratch!

The sounds resonated through the kitchen from behind that door. Beau took off toward the noise that time. He slid into the door because he ran so swiftly toward it. Chandler stood and opened the door, allowing Beau to fumble down the stairs.

"What are you doing?" Shawna asked.

Chandler ignored her and followed Beau.

Kelley and Shawna exchanged glances and followed.

In the basement, Beau barked wildly at the leaded door, charging it again and again.

Shawna grabbed hold of Beau's collar. "Beau, we can't open—

A knock at the front door cut her short. Shawna jogged up the stairs, leaving Beau to his barking.

"She's staying awfully calm through all this," Kelley told Chandler through Beau's growls. "If I were her, I would have moved out of this place by now."

"There's no need to leave," Chandler said.

"What do you mean?"

But before he could answer, Shawna and John came down the stairs, and the banging stopped.

Chapter 20

"We don't know what's inside," Shawna told John, a balding man in his sixties. "We just need it unlocked."

As the caretaker of the estate, John held an oversized keyring hooked to the beltloop of his denim overalls. "Yes, ma'am," he said, searching the ring for the right one. He tried one. The door didn't open. "Wrong key," he said. "My mistake." He selected another and tried again. "That's strange. We'll give 'er the old skeleton key. That should do it." He slid the skeleton key into the lock, but the door wouldn't budge. "I've got all the keys to the house, outbuildings, and lawn equipment, even a second key to your car in case you're locked out of it for any reason. I can't believe I don't have one for this door." In response to Shawna's bewilderment, he added, "Your father made sure you'd be able to get ahold of me to get into your car if you were ever stranded and locked out."

"That's news to me," she said. "But I'll keep that in mind in case I ever do get locked out."

John turned to leave. "I'm sorry I don't have a key for this one, but I can call a locksmith if you'd like."

Shawna followed him. "That would be great—

"No," Chandler said.

"What?" She spun to face him. "What do you mean? Of course we want the key."

Chandler's eyes traveled from Shawna to John and back again. "I just think it would be better if you left it alone until I got back. It'll be safer that way."

"If I may," John said, "that door has been locked for years. I've never been inside, but I know it's not the furnace room. As long as you're in no rush, I can wait to call the locksmith."

"Thank you," Chandler said.

Shawna clapped her hands together and said, "Are you hungry, John? We have a smorgasbord ready to go upstairs."

"As a matter of fact, I am. But I couldn't trouble you. I left Otis outside trimming those rose bushes of yours. I couldn't partake while he works away in the sun."

"By all means, please invite Otis to join us," Chandler said.

"Absolutely," Shawna added.

"Thank you both—all," John said, smiling politely at Kelley. "I'll fetch him."

Shawna, Chandler, and Kelley waited in the kitchen until John and Otis made their way inside. Shawna fried a few more eggs and scrambled a half dozen more. While everyone enjoyed their meals, Beau sat below the table, patiently awaiting a dropped morsel.

"This is all wonderful," John said through a large bite of sausage.

"Feeding you is the least I can do after asking you to come out here this morning."

Little talk followed, except for John's repeating how delicious everything was.

"I'll be sure to get with the locksmith about that key. As soon as you're ready, that is," he said after he'd cleared his plate and wiped his mouth clean. He nodded toward Chandler.

"If it weren't for the damn racket, we would never need to open it," Kelley said. She avoided eye contact with Shawna and Chandler, realizing she'd said too much.

"Noises? What sort of noises?" John said.

Shawna opened her mouth to respond, but Chandler answered for her. "Some creaky pipes in there, it would seem."

"Ah, well, I'll be sure to tell your father about that as well. I'm sure he'd like them looked at."

"No need," Chandler said. "As soon as I get back and we have the key, I can take a look at the pipes myself." To Shawna, he added, "I'd hate to worry your parents."

She didn't know why, but she agreed. "Thank you, John, but Chandler's right. I'd rather not bother my parents with it."

Satisfied, John leaned backward in his chair. "This meal reminds me of my beautiful Rosa when she was still with me. Every Sunday, she would make me a breakfast like this."

"My Maevis, too." Otis spoke for the first time that morning. "I do miss her."

"I miss my Rosa too."

"They're both healthy and young," Kelley blurted.

"On the contrary, young lady," John said, "they're both old and quite gone."

"I mean on the Other Side. We're all thirty, eternally young at Home. You'll both see when you get there. There's no time on the Other Side. Fifty years can pass here but feel like a fraction of a second there. There's no forgetting there, no avarice, no anger. There's nothing there but unconditional love and acceptance."

"Well, I believe we now have full bellies and full hearts. Thank you, Miss," John said. She smiled in return.

"I best get out and tend to them flowers," Otis said. "Thank you for breakfast."

"Of course, Otis," Shawna said. "Thank you for all your hard work."

John stood and pushed his chair in. "Before I go," he said, "I saw a few spots in that basement that could use a coat of paint. Mind if I stop back tonight and tomorrow to get that taken care of?"

"I'd appreciate that very much," Shawna said. "Thank you, John."

Otis tipped his hat as he and John turned to leave. Chandler stood to walk them out.

"See? Now you'll have him here too. Extra protection," Kelley whispered across the table.

"Everything will work out fine, I'm sure," Shawna said, stacking dirty plates and taking them to the sink. "Feel like going to the library today? I have to look for a book on something I'm studying."

"Sure, but let's not be too long. I want to spend as much time around Hottie as possible before he leaves."

"Me too," Shawna said.

A half hour later, the kitchen was clean, leaving no trace of the morning's breakfast, and Kelley and Shawna were backing out of the driveway when the little neighbor girl stepped out from behind a bush at the mailbox. Shawna chuckled lightly to herself.

"What?" Kelley asked.

"I guess I don't have to worry about hurting her if I run her over with my car."

The corners of Kelley's mouth twitched upward, and she said, "Nope. She was in your house last night."

Shawna's eyes widened, but she said nothing, waiting for Kelley to continue.

"I saw her and a bunch of other people, like there was some kind of party going on. At first, I thought it was a dream, but this morning, Hottie mentioned talking to me last night. That was in my dream, too—or what I thought was a dream."

"You didn't bother him and try to—"

"No, I didn't molest him, Shawna. I tell you your house was full of a mob of ghosties and you're worried about me getting into his pants?"

Shawna ignored her and said, "Why does it seem like these things come out of the woodwork when you're around?"

"Those of us who can see them have brighter lights for them to see and follow. It's like we're beacons in the night to them. Wouldn't you want to be around someone who can see you, who knows you're still here when you're lost and everybody else, including your relatives, seems to be ignoring you?"

"I would." Shawna turned into the parking lot at the library. "Are you going to get any books?" She stood from the car, swung her bag over her shoulder, and slammed the door harder than she'd intended.

"Easy, killer," Kelley said. "Something on your mind?"

"I'm seeing ghosts, Kel," she said. "Of course there are things on my mind."

"It'll get better." Kelley sniffed the air when they got inside. "I love this place. It's like a smart girl's playground. What are we here for, anyway? Want me to help you find something specific?"

Shawna shook her head. "I just need a few theology books for school. It shouldn't take me long."

"Are you kidding? Take all the time you need," Kelley said, fingering the spines of books in the New Arrivals section. "Where there are books, I'm happy."

"Where will you be? Looking for *The Kama Sutra?*"

"Nope. I have my own copy at home." She winked and wiggled her hips. "I'll be in the paranormal section. Don't forget," she called in a loud whisper, "Hottie's waiting for us back home."

"Wait a second!" Shawna whispered, eyeing the lady at the desk, Mrs. Sampson, the former high school librarian. The woman was snotty then, and she was snotty now. "Spit out your gum," she mouthed.

Kelley shook her head and blew a bubble, popping it just as she was passing in front of Mrs. Sampson, who scowled and let out a low growl of disapproval. Senior year, Kelley bought a jar of peanut butter and stuck a note to it that said, "Your cats will LOVE this!" with a winky face. She was suspended.

Shawna found three books right away to sit and thumb through. Kelley slammed a stack of seven onto the table and pulled up a chair. They sat at a round table, pens in hand, ledgers out, scribbling notes as they flipped through pages. They sat that way over two hours.

Shawna stretched her neck from side to side. "I think I'll finish these at home," she said. "What do you think?"

Kelley checked the clock on the wall and said, "Deal. Just let me do another quick check." She jog-walked back to the paranormal section. A minute later, she dropped a stack of 13 books on the desk in front of Mrs. Sampson.

Chapter 21

"Oh, we have to go to Instant Karma. Do we have time?" Kelley asked, carrying her stack of books against her hip. It was a Candle Shoppe with incense, sage, and all of the white witchery essentials.

"Drop these off first?" Shawna asked, lifting her books an extra inch.

Relieved of the weight of their library selections, which now sat in two haphazard piles in the back seat of Shawna's car, the girls headed for Instant Karma. The scent of sage and burning candles made Kelley feel right at home. She inhaled the aroma and said, "Now we're talking."

A balding man wearing a gray sweater vest and polyester pants greeted them from behind the counter. Wisps of black and gray hairs stuck out from his ears. "Can I help you find something?"

"I think I need one of everything," Kelley said. "This is my kind of store." She wove through a display of windchimes. "Why do you burn sage and sweetgrass in here?"

"Keeps the undesirables out," he said pleasantly, leaning back in his chair.

"Smart." She fingered one of the chimes, made up of amethyst stones.

Several bulk bins of candles sat against the back wall. A vibrant brunette woman wearing a silk floral wrap was sorting them. "Do me a favor, dear?" she asked.

"Me?" Kelley wondered whether the man at the desk would have been able to hear the woman's request if she'd been addressing him.

"Would you tell my husband he's not putting the candles where they belong? I tried to explain the difference between ocean breeze and freesia to him when I was here, but men don't listen, do they?" She never looked up from the candles.

Kelley's eyes widened.

"And tell him to pay closer attention to the signs and displays for the window. He needs to change them out regularly. I left all of the instructions for him before I left. And tell him I said, 'Happy birthday.'"

Kelley rubbed her chin and kept her eyes down as she walked back to the front counter. "Excuse me," she said. "Your wife said you need to put the candles where they belong and to keep up with the window displays. She said she left you instructions." She looked over her shoulder at the woman, who was smiling and pointing downward, signaling that the man should look down. "I'm guessing the instructions are under your cash register."

For a moment, the man said nothing as tears welled in his red-rimmed eyes. "Is she here?"

Kelley glanced back at the candles again, but the woman was gone. "I don't see her now, but she was here a minute ago. She smelled like lavender."

The man smiled through his tears. "Where was she?"

She pointed to the back of the store.

The man pushed himself up from his seat and shuffled to the back of the store, a black cane in his hand. When he reached the candles, he inhaled deeply.

"She said to tell you, 'Happy birthday,' too."

He closed his eyes and inhaled again. "Thank you, young lady," he said, turning to Kelley.

While Kelley and the man made their way back up to the cash register, Shawna was looking through books at the front of the store. Shawna couldn't hear what Kelley was saying to the old man, but he was nodding and smiling a lot. She figured Kelley was either complimenting him or telling him a dirty joke. Knowing Kelley, it was probably both.

Kelley placed a few things on the counter beside the register.

"No charge," Shawna heard the man say. She placed the journal she'd been flipping through back on the shelf and moved to stand beside Kelley.

"Really?" Kelley asked.

"I insist. It's the least I could do to repay you."

Shawna raised an eyebrow, wondering what she'd missed.

"I'm looking for some help around here," he added while he bagged Kelley's things. "You'd fit right in. And the next time my Isabella shows up, you'll be here to tell me."

"I'd love to be here around all of these nice things!" Kelley said. "When can I start?"

"How's Monday?"

"I have classes in the morning. Can I take the afternoon hours?"

"That'll do for me."

"Shay, are you going to be alright without me or Hottie in the house?"

Shawna nodded. "I have Beau and my neighbors, Jess and Gussy."

"Are you sure?"

"Definitely. This place is perfect for you. Besides, Chandler's only going to be gone for a little while, and you'll be sleeping at my place. Don't worry so much."

Kelley turned back to the man and said, "Do you think we could push my start date back a week—"

"Call me George, and that's okay with me."

Kelley leaned in closer to the man and said something Shawna couldn't hear, then, "Thank you so much, George. I'll see you soon."

Kelley looped her arm around Shawna's and led her outside.

"You didn't have to do that, Kel."

"Sure, I did. Besides, it'll give me something to look forward to. Now let's go see that hunk of a man at your place."

When they sat in Shawna's car, Kelley pulled a candle from her bag. "This one's for you," she said. "It's white, so it goes with everything, and it's purifying."

"Thanks, Kel." She took the candle and held it under her nose. "Did that lady convince you to buy it?" The corners of her mouth turned up in a slight smile.

"I was wondering if you were going to ask me about her."

"Pretty young to be his wife," Shawna said, pulling out of the parking lot.

"That's because she's transcended. She was just visiting. After I delivered her message, she left again. We're all young and healthy on the Other Side. Everyone's thirty there."

"What else did she say to you that I didn't hear you tell him?"

"You heard it all really. She had those instructions for George to follow, but he couldn't find them. She told me where they were. And she said it's George's birthday." She flipped down her visor and checked her teeth in the mirror.

"To have validation that your loved one is okay after they've left the physical body is huge." No wonder he was smiling so much. You made his day."

"I was happy to deliver her message." She thought a moment and said, "Actually, I was a little worried he would have some kind of a breakdown, but he did well."

"And you got a job out of it."

"It's been a good day, right? Books, candles, sage, sweetgrass, and a new job. Feels like Christmas."

Shawna got into the turn lane.

"Where we going, doll-face? Home is that way."

"I want to stop by work and ask Tony for a few days off."

"Good. I could go for a greasy burger and fries."

"Let's do it."

Chapter 22

The lunch crowd filled the diner. Rebecca, another waitress, greeted Shawna and Kelley at the door. "Hey, Shawna," she said. "Here to pick up your check?"

"Actually, we're here for lunch, Bec."

"Snag that booth over there. I'll grab a towel." Rebecca pointed toward a crumb-covered booth in the corner. A young couple and their toddler had just left it.

"Swamped today," Shawna said, grabbing two menus on their way to the booth.

Rebecca came bobbing back across the dining room, her ponytail swinging with her steps. She wiped down the table with one hand and set two empty cups on the table with the other.

"I'll grab a pitcher," Shawna said to Rebecca, who smiled gratefully and bolted off to one of her other tables. "Do you know what you want to eat, Kel?"

Kelley decided on a burger and fries, and Shawna headed behind the counter, where she wrote up a quick ticket for the kitchen and filled a pitcher with ice water.

When she made it back to the booth, Shawna leaned across the table and said, "Rebecca's little sister, Marisa, died last fall, and Rebecca's sure she hasn't gone into the light. Her family called in the NY Ghost Hunters, but they didn't help her. All they did was make shadows and whisper into machines for television ratings. They told her they were going to try to contact her sister, but they didn't even bring a psychic." She leaned back. "She said her mom wants to help Marisa cross, but she also doesn't want her to leave. I guess they have three toy boxes lined up in her bedroom, and those ghost hunters caught a video of a toy vacuum hovering over them, one by one."

"She should probably drop some grains of salt in the toy boxes, just in case it's not the little girl. Something could be masquerading as her."

A bell sounded from the kitchen, and Rebecca came whipping around the corner, two plates in hand. She placed the plates in front of the girls and expertly flipped a bottle of ketchup out of her apron. "Anything else for now?" she asked.

"Actually," Shawna started, "I know it's busy and now's probably not the right time, but I think Kelley might be able to help you."

"Does she want a job?" She blew a strand of hair out of her face and smiled at Kelley. "I could use a busser for tables 8 and 10."

"I mean with Marisa."

Rebecca froze. It was as though everything in the diner began to move in slow motion around her.

"Just be cautious," Kelley said. "Don't talk to her if she tries to engage you in conversation."

Rebecca eyed Kelley, then turned to Shawna. "What is this?"

"Kelley can help, Bec. She has experience."

"What do you mean I can't talk to her? She's my sister. She plays with Audrey every day."

"Is that another sister?" Kelley asked.

She nodded. "She's three." She looked over her shoulder at a large man sipping loudly on a near-empty cup of soda. "Mom even sets a place for her at the table still. Dad's about ready to call the white coats in."

"I can talk to the High Priestess of my coven if you want me to. I'll ask her to come and help me do a Crossing Over Ceremony."

Rebecca pursed her lips and nodded.

"Shawna will get back to you with a date and time."

"You'll have to convince my mom that it needs to be done."

"We'll do our best."

Rebecca wiped her eyes and drug the back of her hand across her nose as she headed for the bathroom. Tony, the owner of the diner, rounded the corner just as Rebecca was coming through and nearly collided with her. "Are you working today, Bec?" he said, motioning toward all of the tables needing attention.

"Sorry. I'll be right back." She kept her face down as she rushed to the bathroom.

"I feel bad for her," Shawna said. "I should stay here and help her out. I can pick up a few tables."

"She'll be okay," Kelley told her. "Don't forget we have to get back to your place soon. Hottie is waiting for us."

"You're right. Beau's waiting, too. Maybe I should get a couple of carry-out boxes so we can head back."

"Not so fast," Kelley said, eyeing the door. Shawna's friend Paul stood just in the entryway, beaming at Shawna. He grabbed a stool from the counter and pulled it up to their table.

"Twice in one week, huh? Can I join you?"

"Sure." Both girls spoke in unison.

"Should we make more room?" Shawna asked, nodding toward the man still standing in the doorway. He'd come in with Paul.

"I don't take up that much room," Paul said, oblivious to the other man. He held both hands up, showing off the black grease that coated his fingernails and reached his elbows. "I'm going to go wash up." He headed for the bathroom, stopping and leaning over the counter on the way to give Rebecca his order as she was entering a ticket into the cash register.

"That guy isn't here for lunch, is he?" Shawna whispered and pointed to the man in the doorway.

Kelley shook her head.

"As you know, I can't tell the difference between living people and dead ones."

"It looks like he had a major trauma," Kelley said.

"What? How can you tell?"

"He's missing one arm and part of his skull."

"Just what I needed to hear at lunchtime. Why can't I see that? He looks perfectly intact to me."

"You've heard of Kirlian photography, right?"

"Maybe."

"If someone loses a limb, it'll show up in a picture of that person's aura. That's why you see him as whole. And that's proof of our spirits' being whole even if we lose all of our limbs when we're in these bodies. People don't understand that no matter what happens to these physical bodies, we are beautiful, healthy and young, eternal spirits. The body dies, but the spirit lives on. I don't understand why they don't get it. Here, were designed to be bodies with souls. On the Other Side, we're souls with bodies. There's no such thing as death of our spirits."

"I'm thinking you're more Christian than you want to admit," Shawna said.

"Let's just agree that there's life after this bad school trip we have to take here. I think that man needs help."

"Are you going to talk to him?"

"I think I should."

"People will think you're talking to yourself. They'll think you're nuts, or if you're looking in their direction, that you're talking to them."

"I'll whisper to him and have him follow me to the bathroom," Kelley said.

"Really? Just leave him be. He's just standing there. You haven't made eye contact with him yet, so he doesn't know you noticed him."

"Yeah, but it seems like he's waiting for me."

"You think he is."

"How do you know he isn't?"

"I don't, but he'll say something to you if he wants your attention and knows you've noticed him."

"Well, I feel bad for him, Shawna. Apparently, he can't find his way to the light."

"I thought someone always comes for you".

"' Maybe he turned away from the light out of fear."

"Maybe he's one you want to stay away from?''

"Or, maybe he's got a message for someone he wants me to give to them."

"Fine. Go talk to your dead guy, but get right back here, and don't let Paul see you talking to yourself."

Kelley stood and made her way to the man. "Can I help you?" she asked. "Do you need help?"

The man didn't answer her. Instead, he stared at Shawna.

Kelley came back and sat across from Shawna again. "Looks like he doesn't want to talk to me."

"Maybe he's deaf."

"I told you any infirmities we had in the physical body don't affect our perfectly healthy spiritual bodies."

"Well, it's good that he didn't need to talk to you. Shawna said. Yeah, I'm kind of relieved. When they're around, especially close to me, I feel what they're feeling and know how they've passed. I can see it."

Shawna shushed Kelley as Paul reappeared from the bathroom.

"What do you want to drink?" Shawna asked him when he sat.

"I thought you were a customer today," he said.

"I am, but we're understaffed, so I'll just help myself."

"Water's fine," he said with a smile.

Shawna and Kelley pushed their plates forward and waited for Paul's meal out of politeness. When Rebecca arrived with his cheeseburger, she placed it gently in front of him and gave a tiny smile before walking off.

The trio ate in near silence. Shawna felt uncomfortable because that ghost was staring at her. She felt like asking him what he wanted, but Paul was there and it was her place of work. She figured one way to make sure she got the time off she wanted was to make her boss think she was yelling at the gumball machines. She rolled her eyes and picked at her fries.

"Paul's coming over next weekend," Shawna said. The thought manifested like a flame. "I'm cooking him dinner."

"I'm thinking I'll be at the Candle Shoppe that day." Kelley leaned in and whispered low so Paul couldn't hear, "The cards are always right."

Shawna's eyebrows shot up, and Kelley snickered.

Paul finished and wiped his mouth with his napkin. "I wonder if they have any cherry pie around here," he said.

Shawna almost spit up her soda. "Ha! That reminds me of when you ate that whole pie at Mrs. Johnson's house." She took another sip and choked on a giggle. Her laughter was contagious. Kelley's face turned red as she tried to control herself. She didn't get the joke, but seeing her friend in near hysterics had her reeling.

"It was an open house, and all of us kids were allowed in there. I thought the food was free."

"It was, but it was for everyone! You could've shared some of it!"

"Well, I know that now." He smirked as the girls wiped tears from their eyes.

Shawna sighed and left the booth to check the pie cabinet. When she came back, she said, "We have half a cherry pie left from last night. Otherwise, there's a full blueberry and a full peach left."

"I don't eat whole pies anymore, Shawna. We'll call that a one-time thing."

Still grinning, Shawna sliced the half pie into three pieces and plated them. She waved Rebecca over and asked her to add the pie to the ticket.

"Let me get that," Paul said.

"You don't have to do that," Shawna said.

"I want to."

"Thank you."

"Yeah, thanks," Kelley chimed in.

He paid the tickets at the counter, promised to call Shawna before he stopped by next weekend, and left.

"I like him," Kelley said.

"I do too." She nodded toward the dead guy still standing in the doorway. "I wonder if he's going to follow us home."

"We'll see."

Chapter 23

"Don't look now, but he's in the backseat," Kelley said.

Of course, Shawna looked. The dead guy was sitting like a statue behind Kelley. By then, Shawna was ready to confront him. "Why are you following us?"

The man didn't answer. Instead, he disappeared altogether.

"He wanted something from me," Kelley said. "I'll figure it out soon. I wish he would've talked to me."

"I hope he doesn't show up in my house tonight," Shawna said.

"Me too. I didn't just see him in here. I felt him. I felt his pain before I looked to see where the feeling was coming from, and sure enough, he was back there. Sometimes, it's hard to tell if it's my own pain or theirs I'm feeling."

"What do you mean? You aren't in any pain normally, are you?"

"No. That's not what I meant."

The two sat in silence for the rest of the ride.

That night, Shawna had the same dream she'd had every night for the past week. She dreamed that the woman from the parking lot, along with many others, were chasing her through that same cemetery until a dark figure popped up out of the ground between her and the people chasing her. It screamed "This mortal can't help you! You are all damned." It spoke that in Aramaic, but Shawna understood what it had said. Circles of flames in the grass surrounded some of the spirits individually. They were each yanked down into the ground by equally red, flaming hands, screaming as they were dragged below the surface. It turned to her and screeched something in a cacophony of words reverberating in her head. She swore her teeth rattled in this dream. Shawna woke up sweating, heart pounding. She got up and got a drink of water, splashing some on her face.

Kelley was restless, too. She was tossing and turning so much that Shawna couldn't go back to sleep the second time she woke up from that same dream. She knew there was some significance to repeatedly having it. She just didn't know what it was. She had, had the usual dreams that you have again and again about when you fall, or the dream we all have about the same house we're in. We know there's a purpose for our seeing the same things, the same rooms, and the dream occurs in the same sequence every time.

"Ouch!" Kelley said face-down into her pillow. "Go away. I won't!"

Shawna considered waking Kelley up but thought better of it. She'd heard that it wasn't good to do that to people, especially when whatever they were dreaming seemed to be affecting them on such an emotional level. The hairs on the back of her neck stood as Kelley flipped onto her back and sat upright, then jumped from the bed and began screaming, "Get out of here! You were not invited! Leave now!" She was yelling at something in the entrance to Shawna's bedroom.

Chandler's eyes shot open. Through his open doorway, he could see Kelley in Shawna's room. She was in a t-shirt and panties, her ample bosom bouncing with each word. She threw her arms up, exposing her midriff as she screamed.

Kelley locked eyes with him, and they both froze.

"What were you yelling at, Kelley?" Shawna asked gently from across the room.

"There's an entity here, Shay," she said, sounding wide awake. "And it's dark."

"It was that board, wasn't it?"

"I don't think so. I think it was already here, but we may have provoked it."

Chandler still stood in his doorway, staring at Kelley. "I'm sorry for waking you," she said, and she shut the door. She sat on the bed and said, "I don't think this has anything to do with that dead guy from the diner, either. I haven't seen him since we were in the car."

"Is it a man?"

"It's just an entity. They can change their appearance to look like a child or someone approachable, but when they're inhuman, they don't have an aura. That's where I have the upper hand."

"So this one has no aura?"

Kelley shook her head.

"It's gone, right?"

Kelley nodded.

"I'm glad you're here, Kel."

"Me too." She rubbed her eyes and said, "We need to sage the whole house again. Yell for your boy toy."

"Why?"

"We need to talk to tell him what's going on."

"I don't want to worry him."

"Trust me, Shay."

Shawna yelled for Chandler, who knocked on the bedroom door moments later, as though he'd been standing in the hallway waiting for his invitation to enter.

"Come in, Chand."

"Wait!" Kelley said. "We're not dressed." She wrapped a blanket around her shoulders. "Don't just say, 'Come in,'" Kelley whispered to Shawna.

Shawna was perplexed. "What the hell else should I say when he knocks?"

"No invitations like that. You never know if the being on the other side is who you're expecting." Kelley opened the door. "Sorry about all that yelling, Hot—er, Chandler."

"Is everything alright?" he asked, standing in the doorway.

"Not really," Shawna said.

"There's spiritual warfare going on here," Kelley said. "And you're not going to be around."

"Spiritual warfare? Elaborate, please."

"I believe there's a bad entity here."

"I told you, you shouldn't have allowed that board into the house," he snapped at Shawna. "You know better than to jeopardize your safety with things like that."

"I saged the whole house," Kelley said. "That meant the board, the planchette, everything. Everything I do, I do with love and respect."

"You mean to tell me that this is all a coincidence now that you've used that board in this house?"

"Not at all, but I don't think that's the sole cause, either."

"We never actually used the board, Chand," Shawna said.

"The planchette was moving when I came downstairs, and I saw your hands on the board."

"It was moving on its own," Shawna said, now defensive. She had expected him to be more concerned for the girls' safety rather than lecturing them like children. "We didn't ask it anything. it had fallen, and we picked it up. That's all that happened."

"Shawna's had issues in the past with entities," Kelley said. "Did she ever tell you about her experiences as a little girl?"

Chandler finally let go of the door handle and came into the room. He sat beside Shawna. "What happened?"

"Which time?"

"Any time."

"One time, at the old house, I was in the living room, watching television at night, and out of the corner of my eye, I saw a figure rounding the corner coming from the kitchen, which leads to the basement, where I assume the figure really came from. He had a bright light around him, and he wasn't made of anything solid. He started coming toward me. I was too afraid to turn my back on him and turn the light on. The lamp was across the room behind me. He reached his hand out like he was reaching for mine, and I freaked out. I ran right through him to where the only light was coming from: the kitchen. I stood with my back against the fridge, waiting for that thing to come after me, but when nothing happened, I started to convince myself that I had imagined it. I reached down and grabbed a bottle of Coke from the floor where Mom kept them in their carton. I was spitting cotton balls at that point. I opened it and felt something behind me. I was too afraid to run, so I sort of–I don't know–willed it to be my imagination. I thought if I ignored it, it might go away, so I focused on my drink. I opened the bottle, and I felt my hair swishing against my back. That thing was messing with my hair, Chand. It flipped my hair three times. One-two-three quick flips. I didn't sleep that night.

"The worst time, I was in bed. I heard my mom coming up the steps to go to bed. I watched for her, and around the banister popped a little girl. She was a neighbor I'd been babysitting that week, but she had died two days before this happened. She started crawling toward me. I sat frozen on my bed with my knees pulled to my chin when she started smiling. Just when I thought she was going to pull herself up onto my bed, she vanished.

"I know there were others, but those are probably the worst two I can remember."

"Wow!" Chandler said. "That must have been hard."

"Do you have to leave already? Can't you wait until all this stuff stops around here?" Shawna asked, leaning her head on Chandler's shoulder.

"I wish I could wait, but it's very important that I go now. I made a promise that I have to keep."

"Well, come back as soon as you can."

"I will."

"Sorry I got you up," Kelley said.

"Don't be. I was already awake," he said. "My cab will be here any minute."

Chapter 24

Chandler asked them to leave with him in his cab, but they didn't. He asked that they not spend the night there until he returned, so after he left, Shawna called Sloane Paxton and asked if Kelley and Beau could come with her to stay at the Paxton's hotel in town for a week or so. Sloane had always been trying to manipulate Shawna into marrying her son, so Shawna wasn't surprised when she was invited to "Come right on over."

"I'm going to jump in the shower," Kelley said, slinging a clean pair of jeans over her shoulder. "Give me ten minutes."

Shawna called John next and asked him to skip the yard work and the painting that weekend. "We'll be back next week," she said while she and Kelley danced around each other in her bedroom, packing their things. "Enjoy your weekend at home." She thanked him and tossed her phone into her bag when Beau suddenly started barking and snarling. Another growl joined his. She turned slowly.

A towering, demonic figure loomed over her. Its flesh reeked of rot and resembled human muscle stripped of its skin. It reached a gnarled, bony hand toward her and held its palm upward as if waiting to be given something.

Shawna stood frozen as Beau barked and lunged toward the figure again and again.

It raised its hand, and Shawna's body levitated before slamming into the wall. It pinned her arm to the wall and ran its snout along her skin, sniffing, then letting out a screech so piercing that it shattered a water glass on the bedside table. Beau cried out.

"Go, Beau!" Shawna gurgled against the demon's force. The demon turned on the dog, dropping Shawna to the floor. Still barking, Beau backed under the bed and hid long enough for the demon to turn its attention back to Shawna.

Beau charged.

The demon threw one hand out, and Beau flew across the room and struck the opposite wall. A gut-wrenching crack rang out, and Beau tumbled into a heap on the floor.

Shawna fought against the demon's grasp. She couldn't breathe, and Beau's painful cries were like a vice on her lungs. Blood was trickling from his mouth. Tears poured from Shawna's eyes as she kicked and clawed at the thing's sticky flesh.

The demon screeched again, and thin streams of smoke whirled around its body. It dropped Shawna again and reeled, revealing Kelley, wrapped in only a towel, standing behind it. She held a bottle of Holy water.

The creature sent Kelley soaring across the room, and she landed beside Beau.

Shawna gasped for air as she crawled to them.

The demon disappeared.

"Are you okay?" Kelley asked, now naked. Wide eyed, Shawna shook her head no. On shaking legs, Kelley retrieved her towel and wrapped herself again.

Shawna staggered to her feet and pulled a blanket from the bed before wrapping Beau in it. She hoisted him as gently as she could, and without another word, hauled him down the stairs.

She didn't say a word for the majority of the drive to the veterinarian's office. Kelley sat in the passenger's seat, still in her towel.

"I don't understand," Kelley said. "Holy Water is supposed to make things like that disintegrate."

"Beau's my only concern right now," Shawna said. She winced every time Beau let out a whimper from the backseat.

When they arrived at the clinic, Beau was taken straight to x-ray, then immediately to surgery. The vet tech came out and told Shawna that Beau had a ruptured disc in his lumbar vertebrae, but more seriously, he was bleeding internally from broken ribs and a punctured lung. She was inconsolable.

The girls sat in silence between sobs and hugged each other gingerly because they were in pain too. Shawna begged Kelley to go to the hospital, but she refused. She was staying right there with her friend waiting for Beau to get out of surgery. Shawna called Chandler and got his voicemail. She told him what had happened. She also told him that they were staying at the Paxton's hotel for the week. Then she called Paul and told him that they were at the vet's and Beau was in surgery, and a visit to her house wasn't going to work that week. She said the reason had to do with renovations going on, and she felt perfectly fine saying that. In fact, it was the truth. That monstrous creature had rearranged a lot in the house. Paul said he'd be right there to sit with them and said he'd bring something hot to drink.

He arrived twenty minutes later with a dozen donuts and three cups of hot cocoa and bottled water. Shawna refused the food, but she took the water from him, tears still streaming down her face. He had noticed the bruises on her neck, but he looked away when she saw him looking. Explanations were in order, but not now. The three of them sat there for hours without speaking.

The doctor came out and said they had stopped the bleeding first thing and set Beau's ribs and bandaged him up. He said the disc would most likely require injections. He recommended them if the disc didn't heal enough on its own over time.

"I don't want to see a dog his age in surgery again unless it's absolutely necessary," Dr. Muntz had said. He recommended massage and acupuncture for Beau's pain. Kelley smiled hearing alternative treatments other than medication being recommended by a doctor. "He might get relief, may not. Dogs handle and hide pain much better than we humans do. In the meantime, no running or jumping. Short term, just a lot of pampering. I'd still try any alternative treatments prior to considering surgery on his spine," he added.

Kelley beamed at the doctor. "Beau will be fine," she said.

"He'll get all the pampering he can take," Shawna added.

A weight lifted from Shawna's shoulders, and tears welled in her eyes. She couldn't wait to see him and bury her nose in his fur.

"You can see him as soon as he's awake from the anesthesia," Dr. Muntz said. "He's a friendly pup, but he did growl at me after surgery. He's never done that before." He shrugged and added, "They tend to stay foggy for some time after anesthesia, though."

Kelley and Shawna glanced at each other. They knew the reason Beau growled. He was still thinking about that creature that had hurt them all. Dr. Muntz told the girls to go home and get some rest. Shawna scoffed. There was no way she was leaving without seeing Beau first. Dr. Muntz apologized again and said it was time for him to check on his other patients.

After a couple of hours, Dr. Muntz returned and said Shawna was able to see Beau. As soon as he saw her, his tail started thumping against his kennel. He tried to stand, but she made him stay where he was. "Stay, Beau," she said, wrapping her arms around him and nuzzling his scruff.

"We'll keep him for at least twenty-four hours, maybe longer for observation," Dr. Muntz said. He showed her the medication she'd have to give him when they got home, and he left them to visit with Beau.

Shawna didn't know whether she still had a home to go back to, but knowing that Chandler would be back soon and Beau would heal quickly comforted her. Even so, she knew she couldn't spend time in that house without thinking of that thing.

In the parking lot, Paul invited Shawna and Kelley to his place to rest until Beau was allowed to go home. Shawna thanked him but declined. "I think I'll take the catamaran out," she said. "A nice, peaceful sail will do me good."

"Count me in," Kelley said.

Paul chuckled. "Have fun. You two can stop by if you feel up to it later on. The Petersons' dock is two doors down. Carly's always on vacation somewhere. You could leave your boat there for two weeks and it wouldn't matter."

"You're sure she won't mind?" Shawna asked.

"Positive."

Chapter 25

On their way to the harbor, Kelley spotted the lights of the fairgrounds. "Can we stop?" she asked, staring at the Ferris wheel.

"Fine," Shawna said smiling, "but only because Beau's stuck at the vet still." She knew he would be fine, but she didn't like being apart from him. At least some time at the carnival would distract her.

When they pulled into the parking lot, Shawna wasn't surprised by how busy it was. The sun hadn't come up yet, and the carnival was still full of late-night revelers from the night before.

The aroma of frying batter wafted around them as they made their way through the aisles of vendors. "We *have* to get a funnel cake," Kelley said.

"I think we do."

As busy as it was, the treat line moved quickly, and in no time, both girls were carrying plates of greasy, crunchy, cakes. By the time they reached the Funhouse, both of their plates were empty.

Seven minutes of dizzying maze travel sent Shawna and Kelley's insides rolling, but they laughed nonetheless. They nearly fell out of the Funhouse exit in a heap of giggles and greasy fingertips.

"Sorry!" Shawna said, bumping into someone's backside.

Chase, the busboy who works with Shawna at the Robin's Nest, spun to face her. She greeted him, but his response was unenthusiastic, not because he wasn't happy to see her or because he didn't like her—truthfully, he had the hots for her, just like every other red-blooded guy who met her.

"I heard about your dad," Shawna said. "I'm sorry."

Chase's dad had passed away the week before. He explained that he had picked up a job as a ticket boy at the carnival to help cover the medical bills left over after insurance paid its share. "I hate insurance companies," Shawna said.

"Me too," Chase said.

Kelley leaned in and whispered to Shawna, "His dad's here."

Shawna turned to Chase and said, "You're going to find this hard to believe Chase but my friend here can communicate with spirits, and she says your dad's here."

"You're right. I don't believe it."

"Your dad's standing right next to you," Kelley said.

"Yeah, right," Chase said.

"Your dad says to tell your mom there's an extra insurance policy in the bottom of the file cabinet on his side of the closet. You don't have to work extra hours, but he's proud of you."

"My dad's here?"

"Right next to you. If he were any closer, he'd be standing on your foot. When I see them, they're usually behind the person they want to talk to if they can be."

His jaw hung slack, and a moment later, he asked, "Can you come home with me and tell my mom?"

"You can tell your mom," Shawna said.

"Your dad will go with you whether you stay and finish your shift here tonight or not. He says that policy is worth a million. He also says there are stocks and bonds that are your mom's now and that he already paid for his funeral and burial plots for him and your mom. All she has to do is call Mr. Blakely, his attorney. He'll help her with the paperwork. It's David Blakely, not Roger. He says his financial advisor is Sheldon Horowitz. Also, at your parents' bank, there's a safety deposit box numbered two-twelve that your mom needs to know about."

Out loud, but seemingly to herself, Kelley said, "Really?"

"What?" Shawna asked.

"His dad wants me to write it all down."

Shawna chuckled and said to Chase, "Your dad doesn't think you'll remember the names."

"He's right. I won't. Can either of you?"

Kelley pulled a pocket-sized notebook from her bag and spoke as she scribbled. "Blakely, the lawyer, and Horowitz, the financial advisor, and two twelve, the number for the box at the bank." She ripped the piece of paper from the notebook and handed it to him. Chase's father nodded his thanks.

When they left the funhouse, Kelley said, "I can't believe anyone can be so daft! Or does he have attention deficit disorder or something?"

"I don't know, but he's a nice guy and a hard worker."

"I'm sure he's nice, but wow, it was two names and a number to remember! But he was probably so overwhelmed with the fact that his dad was with him that he couldn't absorb all the information. I've had that happen more than once."

"There's the Kelley I know! You're not judgmental."

"No, but I get annoyed with all the Q & A at times, and I'm far from perfect. At least his dad wasn't all beaten up. I told you I feel their pain. That dude died of a brain hemorrhage. I have a splitting headache."

"I have Advil if you want some."

"Thanks. I wanted to brew up a natural pain remedy for this weekend. Wanted to see how my stuff works for the pain I've had since the attack before I took any medication. Shawna, there are a lot of spirits here."

Shawna got the back of her shirt tugged just then. She and Kelley turned to see a little boy about seven standing there. Shawna said, "Hi. Can I help you?"

He shook his head yes and said, "Can you help my mommy not be sad anymore?" He was pointing to a woman sitting on a bench by herself clutching a teddy bear, openly crying.

Shawna pointed to Kelley and said, "My friend here will be able to help you both." Kelley went over to the woman, and the boy followed. Shawna stayed back. She saw the woman nodding, crying more, then smiling and crying even more, but to Shawna they seemed like happy tears. It looked too, as if that was the first time she had smiled in a long time. Kelley hugged her. The boy kissed his mommy and she touched her cheek where he had done that. Kelley told her that he just kissed her and she cried more. She stood up and thanked Kelley and gave her another hug. Kelley went back to Shawna. She said, "That boy was a cancer patient. I'm not feeling well, Shay. Can we leave before anyone else corners me? About one third of the people here are spirits."

"Yeah, let's get on the water Kel."

Chapter 26

The girls left and headed to Witcham Bright. Shawna told Dan they were taking the boat out. He noticed both girls had their pajamas on, but didn't say anything. Kelley was able to dress in bottoms and a t-shirt on the way to the vet's office. It was warm enough for shorts with a t-shirt or swim top. Both wore flannel. For all he knew, they could've had swimsuits on under their clothing. Dan reminded Shawna that the Regatta would take place later that day, in just a few hours. All the more reason to stop and see Paul's house. She told Dan that they might not make it back tonight. She explained the invitation so he wouldn't worry about the two out on the open water alone and not coming back all night.

They were almost to the other side of the island when Kelley said, "Don't look now, but we have company." It was a man, well the ghost of a man. He looked like he just came from the bottom of the ocean, complete with a seaweed ensemble. He had a hook for a hand. He scraped the railing and dragged himself toward the girls. Shawna had a hard time concentrating on steering the catamaran with this new stowaway on board. Kelley asked, "How can I help you?" He just kept coming.

Shawna said, "He's using the railing to make as much noise as he can to try and scare us."

"Yeah, no, I'm sure he'd be walking if he had his bottom half."

"He doesn't?"

"Nope," answered Kelley. "Missing an arm, too." She rubbed her arm where his was missing. "What do you want?"

He was within five feet of them when he gurgled, "Aaaaaargh, Duratoway!"

Water spewed from his mouth, and a crab crawled out of his eye socket. He got no reaction from either of them by what he said, so he tried again. "Duratory." He coughed up more water. Kelley pulled out her Holy water and squeezed the bottle spraying the Sea Captain and he disappeared. It hadn't occurred to either of them that he was trying to say a word that Shawna's heard a lot lately, and from those not at rest. Shawna was beside herself with all of this paranormal activity happening around her. To Kelley, it was just another day at the office, but she had some idea of why it was happening now to her friend.

Chapter 27

They reached Paul's house and saw the dock she was supposed to use. Shawna sailed past it, turned around and had come abreft of the dock. She had tied the sails, was prepared to lock the deckhouse, and had done everything she needed to do so she was only steering to the shore. It all went well for her. She was off the catamaran and on the dock with the bow rope. She had given Kelley the one for the stern. She tied the rope to the dock past the bitter end and secured the one Kelley had in her hand standing next to Shawna. She had to admit that she wasn't too cool with the terminology mariners used, but she knew where to tie what to what, and how to get where she was going, and to do so safely. She certainly wasn't an old salt like her father and his friends, but he left the vessel with confidence in her ability to use it safely.

Paul was out in his yard watching her dock. He had walked down there as Kelley had handed the rope to Shawna. After she secured it to the dock, she stood up and turned around to be face to face with Paul. He said, "I'm impressed."

She said, "Don't be. I'm a novice."

"Your dad had to have seen a sailor in you or he wouldn't have left this boat for you." She was going to correct him about calling the vessel a boat, but she knew she did it, too.

He grabbed their bags from the vessel, and led them to his house. This was the house she had wanted to see on the inside that she admired from the catamaran. Shawna was surprised that it was Paul's house. It was even cuter than she'd imagined it to be inside. It looked like a stone Chalet complete with a matching fireplace. She was impressed. He said, "The spare bedroom is all set up for you girls. Maybe you'd like to get in the hot tub before you sleep?"

Kelley said, "No, thanks. The salty water's calling my name. There's a book I have to finish tonight, and I'd rather sleep in the boat. I'll read myself to sleep with the waves rocking me."

"Kelley, you don't have—"

"I want to!" Shawna knew arguing with Kelley was futile. When Kelley had her mind made up, she was doing what she said she would.

"Here's the key to the deckhouse. I'll wake you when I'm ready to go. The vet's office opens at seven during the week. I don't know what time they'll be open in the morning, especially since it's a Sunday, but I'm leaving here at eight."

Paul invited them to dinner first. He had ordered in prime rib, cheesy, potatoes and green bean almandine. He had a Cabernet Sauvignon set up and opened. Shawna gave him points for letting it breathe before pouring any. At the invitation, Kelley said, "You don't have to ask me twice, thanks." They all ate their fill. The girls took turns showering. Kelley went out to the catamaran with a doggy bag full of food complete with a hunk of cherry pie. Dinner wasn't a dinner for Paul without that for dessert at least one day a week.

He and Shawna were alone. "What kind of hot tub do you have?"

"I've got a Caldera, a Martinique."

"That'll work. Kelley should have used it. She's a lot sorer than I am." Her thoughts turned to Beau.

She started talking about him when Paul put his finger to her mouth to shush her. He whispered, "He's fine. We'll get him in the morning. I'm sure he's sleeping off the meds they gave him."

"Yeah, I suppose you're right. I mean, I know he's fine. He's most likely fast asleep now, and we did get to see each other."

"Yep, so stop worrying and try to relax."

Paul took her hand and led her to his hot tub. They kissed a hot, passionate kiss that sent heat through her while they undressed each other. She was ready for him. He led her up the steps and into the spa, his "desire" leading the way. The sexual tension between them was tenuous. He sat in one of the seats and she straddled him, rocking on his hard shaft. He lifted her up and down on him, kissing her fervently from her mouth to her neck to her nipples. He paid special attention to the bruises on her neck. She stood up and bent over the tub, and he entered her from behind. All the while, they kissed. She turned and grabbed his hair, kissing him, flicking her tongue inside his mouth and licking his lips, moaning as she rocked to his rhythm. He thrusted and pumped and got as deep inside her as he could and they remained that way, swaying to their own beat, her rocking her hips against him. He moved with her, and then said, "I, I can't."

"Okay," she said, between her hot, breathless grunts and groans. He climaxed and she felt him throbbing inside her. She moved on him, moaning in his mouth and kissing him. He was moaning too.

Then spent, he sat down and pulled her to his lap and kissed her more. She broke the kiss and said, "Pie?" He answered with a smile. She said she'd shower first and meet him in the kitchen for the pie. He followed her to the shower. She looked back and saw he was ready for her again. She said, "I thought you wanted pie?"

He said, "I do," and got in there with her. She cleaned up and was ready to get out. He grabbed her arm as she reached for a towel, lifted her up on him and set her down on his erection. She was up against the wall in his arms, her legs on either side of his hips, the towel wrapped around his shoulders. He brought her up and down on him as they kissed. She grabbed his ass and dropped the towel, leaving it to soak up their lust on the showers floor. When he was as far inside her as he could be, she held him there. She moved on him as much as she could while being held in the air. She felt herself climax. That's all it took for him. He couldn't take anymore, and he said, "Can I?"

She answered with her mouth against his, "Mmmmhmmmm." He climaxed again. They kissed while she washed his chest, he hers. They washed each other's backs.

After he got cleaned up, she kicked him out of the shower. She had to tend to her personal cleanliness without him watching her. She cleaned her diaphragm and packed it away in its case, and got herself cleaned up and out. When they got to the kitchen, the food was splayed all over as if someone had thrown it against the wall. Shawna saw movement out by the hot tub with her peripheral vision. It was the little girl from her neighborhood! "What-the-get over here!" she yelled. The girl disappeared. Paul was standing right behind Shawna when it happened. He saw her vanish too! Shawna knew he had seen it by the expression on his face when she turned to go back inside. He started to ask her what happened to the girl and she knew it was time to tell him what was happening. She explained it all, including how Beau had gotten hurt, her and Kelley too. She thought he would think she was nuts, but he believed her. He knew about her house on Valley Street and shared his own experiences with her about growing up living by that cemetery. She was relieved that he understood everything. He didn't want her to go back to the house without him. She said that she, Kelley and Beau were going to the hotel to stay while Chandler was away.

They sat and talked over what was salvaged of the cherry pie. She called Kelley's cell, told her about the little girl, and Kelley said, "I knew it! I'm on the right track with my research then."

The veterinary clinic was closed on Sundays, but Shawna knew someone would be there watching the pets. She knew she'd get to see Beau again. And hoped he'd be leaving with her that day. They all peered in the door as Shawna knocked, then pounded on the door. There was a car in the parking lot, so she knew someone was there that early. She saw someone. It was Dr. Muntz. He walked to the door smiling, and let the trio in. He knew better than to tell them to have a seat. Rather, he led them back to where her buddy was. Beau was out of the cage they had kept him in for observation and he was eating. When he saw his mistress, he started for her. She met him halfway. He was barking his happy bark and wiggling. She had him sit to settle him down. She hugged him tightly and he quivered with excitement and contentment at the same time. He then collapsed in her arms with relief. The doctor said he was doing much better than he had expected after the injuries he sustained just the night before. In fact, he was well enough to leave there today, but strenuous exercise was out, nothing but going out to potty, and then a lot of sleeping. He couldn't go up or down stairs, just R &R for Beau. Smiling, Shawna said, with the exception of runs with Chandler or herself, that was the norm for Beau anyway. They all laughed. Beau wagged his tail. Excellent, said the doctor. I'll see him back in a week then.

"Great! Thank you so much, Dr. Muntz," Shawna said. She hugged him, paid the bill and left.

Chapter 28

On the way to the hotel, Shawna said, "Okay, give." Kelley looked in Paul's direction. Shawna said, "It's okay. I told him everything, so now you tell me what you know, please."

"There's not a lot to tell. I just know the spirits are following you around, not me. Your light shines a lot brighter than it used to. I think now that you're aware of their being around you and you accepting that fact, you'll see them more often."

Shawna said, "So, now I'm a lot like you?"

"Yep, sorry babe, but you are."

"Humph," Shawna said. She turned to look at Paul and asked what he thought of it all.

He said, "I always knew you were special. Now everyone else knows it too."

"Good answer," Kelley said.

"Sloane has been expecting us since I called."

"Well, we'll be fashionably late", Kelley said. Shawna didn't find that remark amusing but said nothing. She was nervous about having Sloane think she was taking advantage of her hospitality. She didn't want that.

They got to the hotel. Paul walked in too. She didn't want him coming in with them. He saw her surprised look and said, "I'm getting my own room. Don't worry."

The girls were checking in when Sloane walked up. She snapped her head in Paul's direction because he was in such close proximity to the girls and Beau. He looked away so she thought he wasn't part of their little group. Sloane said, "I'll take care of them, Leanne." The woman looked frightened and stepped aside saying, "Yes, Mrs. Paxton."

"Where's the bellboy?" She started ringing the bell and Karl, the man who held the job, had been talking to the doorman. He heard the bell and saw it was his boss ringing it and hot-footed it over to her.

"Mrs. Paxton, so nice to see you."

"Take these things to the Penthouse, please. These ladies are my guests, as well as the Labrador. Everything is complimentary to my guests, and the dog is to be treated as they will be."

"Yes, Ma'am," said Karl.

"Thank you so much, Sloane. I really—we really appreciate it," Shawna said.

"Of course, dear. It looks like your dog has had an accident."

"Yes, unfortunately, he got hurt. That's why we couldn't come straight here."

Without asking how Beau got hurt or seeming to care, the woman said, "Let me know how the service is, won't you?"

"I'm sure it will be fine," Shawna said.

"It better be," she said as she looked at the girl behind the counter.

The girl gave a nervous smile to her boss and said, "We'll take good care of them, Mrs. Paxton."

"I'm sure you will," said Sloane.

They got to their room and the man deposited their luggage by one of the beds. Shawna tried to hand him a twenty, but he refused. "Please take it. We appreciate your help."

He said, "Thank you Miss," and took the gratuity. "If there's anything you need, don't hesitate to call. The kitchen's open twenty-four hours a day."

"Thank you, Karl."

"Of course, Miss. You ladies have a good night." He left then.

Kelley was thrilled about being in the Penthouse. She jumped up and down on her bed, was going to call Beau up, then jumped down, picked him up, and put him on Shawna's bed. After setting him down gently, she ran to the balcony. "Look at this view! Amazing! Want to order room service?"

"You can get what you want. I'm not hungry." Shawna pulled the crystal out of her pocket and spun it between her fingers, admiring it.

"Fine! I'll order, but I'll get enough for all of us in case you change your mind. Beau, you want a burger or a steak?"

He barked.

"Filet mignon it is, unseasoned, rare, of course. I should've known."

Shawna was preoccupied. She didn't like leaving her home, and Paul was staying at the hotel too. She wished Chandler would get back soon, but then he wouldn't want her seeing another man. She was conflicted, so she didn't think she'd be able to sleep. After she saw the spread Kelley ordered, she decided she'd eat something, and what woman is going to turn down an all you can eat sundae bar wheeled to your room? There were four carts of food for two girls and Beau. Shawna felt guilty. She didn't want the Paxton's to think she was taking advantage of their generosity, and sending a cart back full of food would be rude.

Beau was sleeping off his steak, let alone his meds, so she didn't feel bad leaving him in the room to go down to the pool. She'd been eating so much with Kelley lately and hadn't been exercising. No wonder she didn't feel right. She locked the balcony doors before she left.

When she and Kelley got to the pool, the lights were off, but there was an attendant to turn them on for the girls and open things up. He fired up the jacuzzi, too. After a few laps, she'd use the hot tub. That would help her sleep. Not Kelley. She was all wound up on a sugar high from her triple chocolate sundae with extra whipped cream.

The pool was warm. Shawna dove right in. She felt like she was on holiday. In a way, they were. Shawna spent a half an hour in the hot tub. Kelley was in there before her. She needed it.

Shawna was ready to go back to the room. She told Kelley to stay there if she wanted, but Kelley went with her.

They walked into their room quietly. Beau lifted his head, saw it was them, and went back to sleep. He was enjoying the peace and quiet himself! Shawna slid into bed with him. Kelley got into her own bed too, but read instead of going right to sleep. As much as she loved Beau, she was glad she didn't have to sleep in the same bed with those two.

When Shawna woke up, Kelley was up sitting in her own bed reading. Shawna reached for Beau and noticed he wasn't beside her. She asked Kelley where he was. Kelley told her that the man that brought their luggage up last night had just left with Beau for a walk. Shawna jumped up out of bed and ran out the door, down the hall and caught them at the elevator. Beau saw her and dragged Karl out of there to Shawna. She hugged her buddy and got wet, sloppy kisses. She laughed, and asked the guy where he was taking him, and he said he was taking him to the park across the street to relieve himself. She said, "Thanks Karl, but I'd like to walk Beau myself." They rode down with the man and she took Beau for a slow walk even though he seemed he'd rather run. She was happy that he seemed to be much better than the vet had assumed he would be so soon after his surgery.

When they got back to the room, Kelley still had her nose in a book. Shawna asked her what was up with that. Kelley said it was extracurricular studies. "Then, why here?" Shawna asked.

"Why not? You know I love to read."

"Yeah, I should've brought some with me too, I guess."

"I'll share mine. I could use another set of eyes anyway," Kelley said.

"What are you looking for?"

"Elemental names. Lower level spirit names. A gatekeeper's name. Stuff like that."

"You mean like hell?"

"Yep." Kelley said.

"Okay, I'll help." Shawna got Beau a bowl of water and ordered scrambled eggs, sausage and toast with milk for three.

"So, what's all this about?" Shawna asked between bites.

"I told you I had a feeling about that thing making those noises in your basement. I think it's an Elemental spirit. I've studied where that terminology came from, and then there's the other inhuman entirely. With the Egyptians, there are three classes of rulers: gods, lowercase 'g,'" she said, "heroes, and manes. They're subdivided into seven sections with a deity at the head of each. There are the Elementals that inhabit or represent nature. That's more my arena. Then, there are the even worse inhuman ones, and I think that could be what's in your basement, an Inhuman spirit. You know what that is, right?"

"Yeah, Kelley. I am studying theology. It's an entity that's never lived before, not born of water. A demon."

"Yes, like in your Bible. Now, don't freak out, but I think it's there because of Chandler and you."

"Why us? We're good people!"

"I'm trying to figure that out, and what its name is. When you have its name and speak it out loud, you have power over it. On the flip side, people use the name when they're trying to summon it and give it power."

"And how are you going to do it safely? Where's the fine line?"

"As I told you before, it always depends on the intent of the individual saying the name. If you were trying to exorcise something from someone, then speaking its name gives you power over it. This isn't the case here. As I said, I'm thinking it's inhuman, a demon with a whole separate agenda."

"But why? How?"

"I don't know yet, so I'm reading up on it all again. Knowledge is power. You can help by reading this one and telling me if you find anything about why it would be here on this plain. Something like that, like a spiritual Armageddon or something close to that we're unaware of."

"A second Armageddon, Kelley? Really?"

"Well, one or something like it, prior to the real one, yeah. Or maybe it's here now and we're not aware of it yet. Look for signs in these books."

"I think that's all been covered in class, and why the hell would it be at my house, in my basement if it came to cause a spiritual upheaval?"

"That's what I'm trying to figure out, Shawna! You know I'm a sensitive right?"

"I know you have some kind of weird intuition and you talk to spirits."

"That night I went downstairs and found all those spirits in your house is not the only thing that's happened to me while I was staying there."

"What else have you seen?"

"It wasn't what I've seen that has been bothering me so much as what I've felt and heard. Now that you ask, one night when you and Beau were already sleeping and I got into your bed, I saw a shadow man standing over us by the side of your bed."

"A shadow man?"

"Yes. It's a darker than dark presence, said to be evil, a bringer of bad things, like a bad omen."

"Oh, no."

"Yep. I thought if I turned my back on it, I wouldn't be giving it any attention, therefore no power. It couldn't feed off of my fear. You see?"

"Uh huh."

"I turned my back on it and saw one crawling on your wall like a spider! I called for Hottie and they disappeared. It seems they're deterred by him. Somehow, he protects you."

"He does," Shawna said.

"Yeah, I know, but I mean there's some significance to his being your best guy friend, and his being around all the time, like a protectorate. Okay, the thing that freaked me out even more than that, if you can believe this, was a dream I had, more like a nightmare. In the dream, I was being beaten, stabbed, cut into and bitten. I yelled, 'Stop it,' because that's all I could do, just lie there.

I couldn't move. At first, I couldn't speak, nothing, but lie there and be assaulted."

"I remember that night! I thought you were griping at Beau about his hogging the bed and farting."

"No! I thought I heard you talking and I said, 'What?' Do you remember?"

"Yeah, I was sleepy, but I remember you turned on the T.V."

"No, I didn't Shawna! I heard that too! It was a conversation of at least two, maybe three entities going on in your room while we were in bed! I thought you were sleep talking when I asked you what you said."

"I was asleep, but I heard you yell, 'What!' You were so loud that I woke up for a minute."

"Well, I was scared, confused, and mad, Shawna! They thrive on all of those emotions! When you're calm or ignore them, that makes them powerless. Anyway, those were not good spirits. I'm telling you, there's something going on that's related to those noises coming from your basement, and your stud knows more than he's saying!"

"Why would he leave me there then?"

"I don't know, but he's definitely no coward. As I told you, I'm looking for answers, so start digging, please."

They spent the whole day reading. Shawna took breaks to take Beau out. Kelley took him once so Shawna could concentrate on a book she had almost finished. They had huge piles of notes cluttering their work area. The last time Shawna took Beau out, she stopped at the store and bought a few packs of pens and ten notebooks figuring if they didn't use them now, she'd use them for classes later on.

Chapter 29

When she got back, they were ready to head to the library for more books and take a short break from reading after that. They headed out with Beau and stopped at a new restaurant by the library. They sat outside on the patio. Turns out, their friend Tyler Owens owned the restaurant and Beau was no trouble. And if there wasn't anyone in there, he would've let him inside. He just loved Beau, and had never seen a dog so well behaved, so calm, even around other dogs that didn't behave like him! They were content with the bistro table on the patio. Beau was happy with any situation as long as he was with his Shawna. They had lunch. Tyler brought Beau out a bowl of steak scraps. That dog was at home wherever he went. He had friends all over town. Shawna was sure everyone liked Beau more than her, and that was alright with her. He deserves five-star treatment wherever he goes. She patted him on the head. He looked up at her with such adoration, such love.

She said, "I love you too, sweetheart. You're the love of my life!" He wagged his tail, gave her a sweet flick of a kiss on her nose, and finished his bowl of food. Then, he drank some of the ice water Tyler had brought out for him. Full belly, thirst quenched, he took his usual position under the table at the girls' feet while they planned the rest of their night. They decided they'd drive by her house after the library. Outside it in the car, they saw lights going on and off. They heard what sounded like furniture getting thrown, dishes being smashed, wood splintering and doors being opened and slammed shut. It sounded like a fight going on in there. Not a good time to grab any clothes they might have wanted and had forgotten to pack when they left. Kelley said, "Sounds like spiritual warfare."

Shawna said, "I've gotta stop at Jess' and tell him to not go in there, that I'm not home. I'll tell him no matter what to stay out of there. I don't want anything happening to him or Gussy!"

When they went to his house, he didn't answer his door, but they heard Gussy barking when they knocked. Shawna was beside herself with worry. She was afraid he had gone to her house and was now being assaulted. She called his phone. He answered after ten rings. *Thank goodness for old landlines!* thought Shawna. She told him that she'd be gone for a week and said if he hears anything coming from her house that it was just Chandler doing some demo. She didn't know what she was thinking telling him that, because Jess couldn't hear a bomb going off right next to him! At least she kept him away from there with him knowing she wouldn't be there. He and Gussy were safe! She had accomplished what she wanted to. While she hated lying, it was for a good reason. Now, her thoughts turned to Paul. He's probably wondering why she hasn't called him when they're staying at the same hotel. More importantly, was Chandler's coming back home. She called and got his voicemail. She left him a brief message telling him that Beau was doing great, they were all fine and she couldn't wait until he got back, and for him to call her. The phone hung up on her. She called it back. She gave him her room number and the hotel's number in case her cell wasn't charged.

Chapter 30

Kelley said, "The cards are always right! You're worrying about everyone, but yourself! You're a nurturer."

"What woman isn't, Kel?"

"True," Kelley said, "but they pegged you. It wasn't just that card, but all that describe you to a tee. You know it's true."

"Yeah, Okay," Shawna said, "Are you thirsty? I thought we could stop and get some ice water and maybe a hot cocoa."

Kelley giggled.

"I'm thirsty, okay?" exclaimed Shawna.

"Yeah, that sounds good, Shay. Then you should call Paul, or better yet, go to his room!"

"No! I'm not going to his room! People talk. Sloane would hear about it, I'm sure. She's bound and determined to get me and that son of hers together."

Kelley suggested that she get her own room and Shawna invite Paul to hers. "That still wouldn't look good!" Shawna protested.

"Why couldn't he just be a friend visiting you? And, I'd be there sometimes. Or, maybe he's the vet checking up on Beau?"

"I don't know, Kelley. That's a little farfetched."

Frustrated, Kelley said, "Vet's make house calls. People are going to talk no matter what you do! You're an adult! You can do what you want!"

"I suppose you're right, but I can't possibly ask for another room."

Kelley said, "Have credit cards, will travel," as she whipped out a slew of cards in plastic sheathing and held them up like a proud grandparent whips out their grandkids pictures. Shawna smiled. Kelley said, "I'll go shopping and of course, hit the library, and maybe even stop and see Tyler and grab a drink there. Then, I'll hang out at the hotel's bar. Maybe a guy will get lucky tonight."

"Well, you be careful, Kelley!"

"I'm always careful!" She whipped out as many condoms as she had credit cards, and in the same fashion.

"You know what I mean!"

"Yes, I know. Only the ones without the tan line where their wedding rings supposed to be. Or, the boys that are obviously there with fake I. D.s!"

"Not funny, Kel!"

"I got it. Don't worry."

Now Shawna was mad.

"How am I not supposed to worry about you with the way you talk?"

"Sheesh, you're as bad as my mom! I'll call you when I get to my room. I'll let it ring twice, hang up and call again. I'll even call my mom!"

"Just text me!" Shawna said with an eye roll.

Now, you're talking my language. Okay, a text it is."

"I'll text you, too, and let you know when he leaves whether that will be tonight or tomorrow morning."

"Oh Shawna, I think I'm rubbing off on you."

Shawna smiled and said, "Yeah, you just might be."

As their conversation wound down about who was sleeping where, they had gotten back to the hotel and were entering their room. Kelley grabbed a bag she had already packed with her toiletries, pajamas, and books. Shawna wasn't surprised. "I'm heading out now," Kelley said.

"Okay, see you tomorrow then. Kiss."

"Back at ya, babe."

Kelley left thinking she was going to get a hot review of Paul's sexual prowess, but Shawna had no intention of sleeping with him here at the hotel. She dialed Chandler's cell. It went to voicemail again. She said, "I miss you too much. Get home as soon as you can please. Love you." She had spoken quickly trying to get all she had to say said before the voicemail ended. Success!

She called Paul and told him she was in the Penthouse suite. She ordered up room service for two. The person on the other end asked. "Not for three?"

She said, "Yes, sorry, for all three of us." She was so distracted with Kelley having left and the idea of being alone with Paul in her room that she was ordering just for Beau and her, not Paul too, and he was on his way. She asked for cherry pie for dessert. She turned on the radio, sat, and waited. No special preparations were made. She really didn't want him in a private room. She wished she would've just met him in the dining hall. Too late now, but she was sure he'd respect her wishes and be a gentleman. She relaxed and opened up a bottle of champagne and poured two glasses of it and set the bottle back in the bucket to chill. There was a knock at the door. She said, "It's open. Come in." It was room service. Paul was standing behind him. Now they knew a man was visiting her! Whether she had him leave in an hour or ten didn't matter. It didn't look good either way. She said, "Paul, our books are at the table. I'll be with you in a minute." She was proud of herself for thinking of that when the help was there, then again, embarrassed that she had to make that up to make herself feel better. Paul played along and sat at the table, which was nice of him. She felt herself flush red as she was seeing the person out that brought their dinner. She added, "He could take the cart with him when we're done with our studies."

"Very good, Madam. Yes, studies."

She said, "Yes, studies!"

The waiter said, "It is customary for us to come and get the cart when you're done with it, Madam."

Shawna said, "Thank you. That will be fine." She closed the door, and didn't want to look at her study partner.

He said, "Now, I feel like a sneaky teenager."

"Well, sorry, but I have to keep up appearances. The owners are my parents' friends. You remember the Paxtons?"

He shook his head.

"Never mind. So, how was your day?"

"Great, but I ran into this chick I used to know a couple of weeks ago and had seen a few times since. We had crazy hot sex a few days ago, and now she invited me to her hotel room to study, I guess." She smiled. He picked up a book. "*Modern Wiccan Rituals?*" Then, with the other hand, he continued to read aloud the other title. "*Deities of the Underworld?*"

"Those are Kelley's," Shawna said. "She's out at the moment having a cocktail so we could be alone."

"I knew I liked that girl the minute I met her."

"She won't be gone long."

"Relax, Shawna."

She said, "Let's eat. I ordered chicken picatta, mashed potatoes, side salads, and da, da, da, da!" She lifted the cloche, "Cherry pie for dessert. A whole pie. Whipped cream on the side, too."

"Awesome! I could think of some creative ways for that pie and whipped cream to get into our stomachs."

"Not here, Paul," Shawna said.

"Then maybe after dinner, we could take Beau for a walk. I see you ordered for three." He served Beau after he gave her a plate of food. He even gave him a piece of pie. She giggled. Paul said, "You want whipped cream with that, Beau?" Beau barked.

Paul squirted whipped cream all over Beau's pie and mashed potatoes.

"Easy with that! He's going to get fat! He's been eating nothing but people food and hasn't been active lately. You know why."

"Oh yeah, sorry." They say the way to a man's heart is through his stomach, but the way to a woman's heart is through her kids or dog. Shawna was sure of that. He left a very good date impression on her.

After they ate, she opened her door and left it that way. She called down for them to come and get the cart, and like a good actor, Paul was at the table studying, writing notes with his nose in a book. He was doing such a great job of it that the waiter bumped the cart on the doorway leaving and quietly apologized. She shut the door, ran to her bed, cracked up laughing into her pillow, and threw one at him. He acted annoyed like he was really into what he was reading. That was even more endearing to her. She walked over to him and said, "You've got a little whipped cream right there," and pointed to his mouth.

"Where?" She kissed it off of him. The kiss got mutually passionate until Paul popped one eye open, looked at Beau, and while they embraced, he reached for Beau's leash. Beau wagged his tail. Paul broke the kiss, and said, "Okay, let's go, "as he clipped it to Beau's collar and pulled Shawna out the door and down the hall to the elevator with Beau leading the way.

It was a cool night, and she didn't have a coat. He gave her his sweater and they walked and talked for a good hour. She was happy because they were out of the hotel room. Her happiness was short lived, however, when she saw the same spirit that was at the diner the day she, Kelley, and Paul had lunch together. He wasn't alone, either. He had five others with him. Should she tell Paul her fears? She thought she had said enough.

"Who's that?" Paul asked.

"What? Who?"

"Oh, never mind. Thought I saw someone. Must be seeing things." She had hoped he'd seen them too, but nope. He wasn't as crazy as she felt she was. He said, "Let's get back inside." She agreed. They were followed back to the hotel.

"See you in the dining room in the morning?" asked Shawna.

"I hope," said Paul.

"Goodnight then."

"Goodnight, Paul."

That was fun. Very PG. She looked at Beau and said, "You like him too, don't you?" Beau barked his approval. "Good," she said. She texted Kelley and said, *He'll be having bfast here at the hotel.*

Way 2 go grl. Mine's eatn now.

Ur sick.

And?

After ur shwr u can come back 2 the room.

Oooh a 3 sm

Ur demented. He's stayn @ hotel while we're here. Will c him 2mrw 4 bfast

K. See u soon

Kelley finished her margarita, shut her phone off, and grabbed her purse and wrap. The only luck she had tonight was being left alone by all these fox-trotting old men, except one fifty-something, pedophile-looking, rug-wearing dirt bag in polyester. She was happy to be leaving the bar. No hot, young guys here. The youngest ones were at least in their forties or late thirties. She could've hooked up with one of them, but he wasn't her type. Besides, she saw the telltale indentation on his finger where his wedding ring was supposed to be. *Another dirt bag!* she thought. She couldn't wait to get back to the comfort of the room and get in her jammies. She had books to read, her first love, but that could wait until morning. She was more like Shawna than Shawna herself realized. She wished she would have rented a room. It was a long way to the top floor even in the elevator. She was tired. She talked a big show but didn't do much, but she amused her friend. Hell, she cracked her own self up!

Uh-oh, spidey senses tingling.

Kelley made her way to the front door and stood by the doorman and looked out onto the street. He told her how lovely she looked tonight. She slurred, "Thank you. I'm Kelley."

"I'm Bernard. It's nice to meet you."

She saw the same spirit from the diner with like sixteen others, maybe it was eight. As much alcohol as she'd had, she couldn't tell. In his face, nearly nose-to-nose, she said, "I'm purty popular tonight, Baarnaaar." She smiled and fought to keep from swaying.

"Yes, you are, Madam." She patted him on the head and walked away as dignified as she could after the drinks she'd had and in stiletto heels and a too-short dress on. Every few steps, she'd have to pull it down. Her straps would fall too from her shoulders. She swore she looked like a hooker! Kelley called over her shoulder, "Baaaaarnaaaaaaaar, do Iiiii loooooouuuuk liiiiiiike aaaaaah hhhooooooookuuur?"

"Of course, not Madam." She mumbled her thanks as she stumbled into the elevator, her heel getting caught in the crevice she would have stepped over any other day. *No wonder I don't meet nice guys!* she thought. And, no wonder that guy at the library kept saying, *No, no, no, no, no,* when she wanted him to get a book down for her! She never got to spit out the whole sentence! He didn't let her! Shawna would think that was funny. She would try to remember to tell her. But now, she had to tell her about the spirit following her again, and bringing backup.

Chapter 31

She got to the door and knocked instead of digging out the key. She was too tipsy to rifle through her purse. Shawna checked the peephole, saw who it was, and grabbed Kelley's arm. She said, "Get in here," as she hauled Kelley in. Kelley tripped over her own toes in those strappy heels. "Didn't get a room, huh?"

"Nope." She fell back on the bed and kicked off the shoes, but they were still attached at the ankle. "Help me, Shay."

Shawna unbuckled her shoes and said, "So, you hooked up with a sleaze ball tonight, huh?"

"So whaaat ifff Ihhiiigh didddd?"

"That's your business. I just hope you didn't make him think there was going to be a second date."

"Yoooddddddddoooooooooooknnnnnnnoooooooooowahm eeeeeeeeellllllliiiiiiiaaaahhhhhhkuuuuuuuuuuutttttttthhhhhhhhiiiii iiiiiiikuuuuuuuuddddddddoooooooooooShawaaaannaaaaliiiiiiiviiii iinssssttttttonnnn (emphasis on the t's) Shananana hey hey hey. Hahahaha!"

"I thought—"

"No, no, no. no. no. Ha! Thatz wha heeeee sayad hahahahaha!"

"Okay, you can tell me in the morning." Kelley wretched. Shawna got the wastebasket for her. She threw up in the basket on her way to the toilet, bumping into the walls on her way. It sounded to Shawna like nearly all alcohol. Smelled like it, too. "Gross," she said out loud. "Leave that can in the bathroom and close the door after you dump it in the toilet." Kelley staggered out of the bathroom with the garbage can and fell into bed. Shawna took her wrap and purse, covered her up, kissed her on the forehead, and said, "Night, bull shitter."

She got in her own bed with Beau and cut the lights. They slept, Kelley not so well, but she did get some shut eye. When she was out, she was snoring, drooling, belching, and farting more than usual. Shawna was disgusted and amused at the same time. Neither of them got a good night's sleep because of Kelley's nocturnal emissions.

When Shawna got up, she tried to be quiet. She turned on the T.V. with the volume down low. She opened the balcony doors to let fresh air in and clear out the smell of alcohol and bile from the room. She'd have the maid service in to clean the room when Kelley was up. Shawna went out on the balcony, looked over the railing, and saw those spirits standing there looking up at her. She'd tell Kelley about them when she woke up. Shawna called down for room service. She ordered Danishes, eggs, bacon, and mimosas. Kelley probably needed a little of the hair of the dog that bit her. She was pretty sure of that. She thought a minute and ordered Bloody Marys too. Yep, that would work.

At the knock of the door, Kelley sat up. lipstick smeared across her cheek, eyes clenched shut, hair a mess. She plopped back down and was out in a matter of seconds. The man came in and pulled Kelley's books out from under the bottom of the cart. He said, "The lady left these here in the bar last night."

"Thank you so much," Shawna said as she took them from him. She thought how sweet Kelley is and what a great friend too. She knew the girl wasn't out on the prowl, rather, she went to the library and stayed down in the hotels bar to give Shawna and Paul privacy. Aaaaw. And she stayed away so long that she drank too much. She should've had something non-alcoholic and not dressed like a tramp. She tried to make Shawna think she had big plans when she didn't have any at all. *How cute!* thought Shawna. Shawna heard a loud long belch. She looked over and saw Kelley's eyes open. She said, "Okay, party girl, time to put something in your stomach other than alcohol." She gave Kelley her books she left at the bar and sat down on her bed.

Kelley said, "Yeah no, there's nothing in my stomach now and that's the way I want it for this morning. You figured me out, huh?"

"Yep! You're my sweetest best friend, and I appreciate what you did. But dude, you should have hit the gym or swam instead of sitting at the bar waiting to come back and sleep."

"Well, a margarita sounded good. Been craving one since that night I asked you for one. Guess I got carried away."

"I'd say so," Shawna said.

"Well, I've got news for you. Creepy dead guys hanging around here now."

"Yeah, I know."

"You do?"

"Yes, saw him last night when Paul and I walked Beau. He was following us!"

"Oh!" Kelley said. "I see."

"What? What do you see?"

"Hang on. I've gotta pee," Kelley said.

"Tell me what you were thinking! What do you see?"

"Hang on. I've really gotta go."

"Take your puke bucket with you and dump it again. And rinse it out, please."

"Gross," Kelley said.

"You're telling me!" Shawna said. Kelley got all cleaned up and cleaned the garbage can thoroughly and the taste of bile and alcohol out of her mouth. Minty fresh, clean, and smelling of soap, hair products, and body wash, she came out with a towel on her head.

Shawna handed her a couple of ibuprofens and a Bloody Mary. "Oh, no, no thanks. No more alcohol."

"Hair of the dog that bit you," Shawna said.

"No thanks. I'll just have a piece of toast and a gallon of water."

Shawna laughed and said, "Okay, now tell me what's up then."

Kelley said, "I have to do more research. I'm not going to jump to conclusions. I don't want to freak you out, either."

"But?" Protested Shawna.

Kelley continued, "As soon as I figure it all out, you'll, of course, be the first to know. Besides, we're hanging out every day now, so don't worry. If there was something I thought you needed to know now, I'd tell you. And yes, when I see ghosties, I'll tell you. I need an ice pack."

"Okay, I'll call down for that, more ice, towels, and a bottle of Advil."

"Wow, it still smells like puke in here," Kelley said.

"I was going to have housekeeping come up a little bit ago, but I didn't think you'd want to hear a vacuum or smell the chemicals they clean with."

"Good, thanks."

Kelley sat at the table and pulled out a book. She got her reading glasses out, threw her hair in a messy bun, and started reading. "You look cute with those on and with your hair like that. Very librarian-ish," Shawna said.

"Thanks."

"Which book do you want me to research first?"

"I got these from the library last night," Kelley said. She pointed to a pile of books on the floor by the table. There must've been like twenty there. Shawna was impressed but at the same time, overwhelmed. Kelley saw the look on her face and said,

"Don't worry. I'll go through most of them. Just grab a couple, please." She did. She got *Modern Theories of the Biblical Text*, and *Allah Allah* something or another. She couldn't read the whole title. Kelley saw the perplexed look on Shawna's face as she was studying the cover and said, "Yeah, I'll take that one." Pointing, Kelley said, "Why don't you grab that one in Latin? You're a good study. I'm sure you'll get through it quickly."

"Okay. I've gotta take Beau out right now, though."

"Okay," Kelley said.

"We'll be back as soon as we can."

"See you soon."

Shawna took a different route out of the hotel, walking Beau through the kitchen. The head chef wasn't happy about that at all. He started griping but got quiet when his sous chef whispered something to him about them being his boss's special guests.

The ghosties hadn't surrounded the building yet. She still had to get him exercise whether they were around or not. She wasn't about to utilize the rooftop terrace with the faux grass for him. That wasn't fair. Nope! They'd go for their walk. Then, she'd sit around and read. Her buddy came first.

Chapter 32

Chandler was uneasy on the plane. He did not like this feeling. He was never uncomfortable in his own skin—well, this meat suit. Although it resembled him as closely as it could, he hated the maintenance of being in a body again. And, how ridiculous it is to take a form of transportation to get where you wanted to go! At Home, you'd think yourself there, and you'd instantly be there. If you wanted a new look, you'd assume it.

This was his fourth flight already and three days in on his traveling schedule here. He bowed his head. *Father, give me the strength to attain my goal and help this child of yours Father, I pray in Yeshua's precious holy name. Thank you, Father. Amen.*

Chandler opened his eyes to a flight attendant who was face to face with him. She said, "Would you like a pillow, sir?"

"No, thank you."

"Water, soda, chips, peanuts?"

"Thank you, no."

"Here's a menu of what we have on board." He saw her eyes behind her glasses were not her own.

"I'm fine," he said. He knew they were closing in on him. He felt it. This must be what that mortal Kelley talks about when she refers to her "spidey senses tingling."

Chandler had already been to England. Buckingham Palace wasn't the easiest to get into with the guards standing outside the gates. There were guards on horseback everywhere, too. The foot guards were nearly the hardest to evade, but the Queen's guard were his biggest concern over all. He had to get into the Queen's private quarters and the Coronation room without getting caught. He could charm the guards and make them sleep, but where was the fun in that? The smartest way in was to wait until the Queen was out of the palace. He had to bide his time. There was a parade later that day, the perfect opportunity for him. He knew he'd have to get in by way of horse guards. That was an entry that was guarded from ten a.m. to four p.m., but even with the changing of the guard, there were still two men on horseback waiting there, watching, while one man replaced another for duty between a four-hour period, between four and eight p.m. He'd have to charm the horses and make them run from the entrance. He might get some men in trouble, but he had to do it to get what he needed.

At six that evening, he did, and the horses ran like wildfire out of the gates. There were sentries bucked off, running all over, chasing the horses. One horse was trying to mount another gelding. *They all should have been geldings*, he thought, but what a show! The men's bear skin caps were hanging off of their ears like feed buckets. He wished he could pull up a chair. This was better than that television the girls watched at home.

He made his way into the Palace and looked for the relic in the Coronation room. Then, he checked the Queen's quarters while she was out with the queen's guard. No luck. He knew he didn't have much time left here. They'll be checking every room, everything before she gets back. There was always someone at the palace for security reasons, but he managed to slip by those people. He even searched the Chapel. Now, he knew he had to either give up looking here and head to Scotland, or cause another fiasco so he wouldn't be seen leaving the castle grounds if he happened to stay past the time of the Queen's return.

He decided to leave. He hopped the flight to Scotland. He looked around and saw a sea of black, soulless eyes staring in his direction. Almost half of the passengers were inhabited by demons. He was surrounded by evil. The humans on the plane were asleep. He knew they wouldn't make a move in front of any humans. Any noise would wake them, and the flight attendants that he had contact with on this flight were humans. They were up by the cockpit. Forty-five minutes left, he thought. He was thinking of a quick way off of the plane when it came to a stop. They landed, and he managed to push his way to the front of the humans leaving, the evil ones glaring at him. A car was parked on the runway. A man was standing by it waiting for someone coming from his plane. He ran to the man. Luck would have it, the man was waiting for him.

They jumped in the car and took off, the demons running after them. When they were a far enough distance away, the man introduced himself as Conor Flannery, a soldier in the Order of the Knights Templar. He said, "I've—we've been expecting you for a long time."

"How'd you know it was me you've been waiting for?"

"I have the second sight, and your medallion would give you away around any of us."

"Well, I'm glad you were there. Thank you."

"Of course. Are you an Angel?"

"No, I'm not."

"There's something special about you."

"And you," Chandler said.

"I suppose if you were an Angel, you wouldn't need my help, but they can't fly or disappear in front of a group of humans."

"No, they can't." Conor was looking at Chandler deep in thought when Chandler said, "Conor! Road!"

He swerved back onto the road, and said, "Sorry, there's something about you that I know is different, though. I'll figure it out."

"Okay," Chandler said.

"Damnit man! Why don't you just tell me?"

"There's nothing to tell, really. I am on a mission, as you are."

"I'll just have to settle for that answer, I suppose."

"Please do. Do you have ideas as to the relic's whereabouts?" asked Chandler. Conor told Chandler one of his brothers in the Knights Templar's theory of how the Stone of Scone (Scoon, as the English call it), was on an island called Vanuata. "There's a tribe there that thought the British royalty were like gods. They would hide it there in a church."

Chandler said, "I've been there already."

"Why would you go there instead of Scotland or England?"

"I went because the obvious places are usually the last place it would be."

"True," said Conor. "And smart."

"Now, this is the last and most obvious place for it to be unless it's been stolen again," Chandler said.

Conor said, "We've been following Jacob's Stone since it came to the States, and I'm sure it's here in Scotland. My question to you is, how are you going to get it from point A to point B without getting caught?"

"I don't need the whole stone, only part of it," Chandler said. "The chosen one only needs that and the selenite crystal she now covets to do what she came here to do."

Connor exclaimed, "I didn't think it would happen in my lifetime! I'm so happy I can help. The brothers are awaiting word from one of us stationed at every International airport around the world, and I'm the one that has the Angel to complete our mission."

"I'm not an Angel, Conor."

"Well, you're as close to one as I'll ever see."

"I'm not that different than you. It's just that this is my fifth time here, and I remember it all. I will tell you in one of my times here I was the first and last Grand Master in your order."

"No way!"

"Yes, I was Jacque De Molay."

"Really?"

"Yes. I held that title from twelve ninety-two until I was executed in thirteen-fourteen."

"The men will be so happy to meet you, Jacque."

"Chandler, please. It's most likely not your first time here either. You just won't remember until you get Home all the lifetimes you've lived, the people and pets you've had with you, who are waiting for you and still love you. It's been probably half a century for you here on this plain, but there, it's less than a heartbeat in time. It's almost like you just left. Time stands still for us at Home."

"How'd you know how old I am?"

"Lucky guess is all. I'm probably off by a month or two."

"I'll be fifty-one in four months. Pretty good guess if you ask me," said Conor.

"Well, I've been fifty in three of my lifetimes, and I am happy to say, I'll be going Home to stay at this age."

"How old are you?"

"I'm infinite, thanks to our Lord's sacrifice on the cross."

"I meant when were you first born?"

"I was first here back around the time of Jacob. My ancestor Myaletis was a Greek nobleman and mercenary that helped Joshua get the Stone through Egypt after Jacob had it. I don't know if he knew if it was stolen or not, but I am atoning for that. I've been here many times. We all take around a one-hundred-year break from coming back here to this plain and enjoy the peace, love, family, pets', and friends' company on the Other Side."

"Huh. How old is that body you're in now?"

"Thirty-two. We're all this age when we're back Home where we belong."

"Huh?"

"I mean thirty, exactly thirty," Chandler said.

"Why thirty?"

"Why not? It's the perfect age to be, forever young, healthy, and mature enough."

"That's the greatest thing I've ever heard!"

"Well, there's so much more to look forward to."

"Can't wait."

"You should worry about how this life is going. Learn what you can so you won't want to come back to learn anything else. Do as much good as you can. Help people and animals, our pets and wildlife, and then you will go Home with no regrets. Love well."

Conor said, "I won't be coming back for any reason"

"That's what we all say, but at Home, where time stands still, we figure a little trip away to learn for God will be no trouble until we're here and experience all the negativity this plain has to offer."

"Do you want to see any of the sights Scotland's famous for?" Conor asked.

"No need. We have the same topography from every country, every nation at Home without all the buildings, the hatred, sadness, the evil here. If I want to visit a beach in Hawaii, I think myself there and I'm there. If I want to visit Scotland's Highland's, I go there. There is no place off limits at Home, and we can live wherever we want. Nothing rivals the beauty of the Other Side.

Mouth agape, Conor said, "Well, I look forward to going Home."

Chandler changed the subject then. He said, "The last known public information about the Stone was that England gave it back to Scotland in Nineteen-ninety-six." They both knew it initially went from England to Ireland, then to Scotland. Chandler wondered if his trip would be prolonged and thought if he couldn't find the relic in Scotland, maybe it was returned to the Holy land from where it originated. He just knew he had to get to it and get a part of it back home to Shawna as quickly as he could.

Chapter 33

Shawna and Beau got to their suite in forty-five minutes. Kelley the bookworm hadn't left her spot at the table. She had already been through two more books. Shawna picked up the Latin book wondering what Kelley wanted her to find in THAT! She asked her and Kelley told her to look for names of evil beings and words used to dispel them, so she did just that. After poring over that book, she gave it back to Kelley who also wanted to thumb through it. Shawna went through five more, taking notes over a three-hour period. Kelley blew through ten in that time. The girls completely forgot about breakfast with Paul. It was lunchtime now. Shawna hoped he didn't leave angry with her thinking she purposely didn't show up in the dining hall because she didn't want people talking. After thinking about the times they've spent together, she knew her thoughts were ridiculous. She called his cell, apologized and invited him for lunch in her room. He hadn't gone anywhere and said he'd be happy to have lunch. She told him it would be a foursome, this time including Kelley. He happily agreed. She was more than happy to have him back in her room with Kelley there and all the books and paperwork spread out when their lunch would be delivered. She ordered Italian beefs with au jus and pepperoncini's, waffle fries, fresh fruit on the side, Cokes and Dr. Peppers, and cherry pie for dessert. She ordered two pies with a spray bottle of whipped cream.

Paul showed up again with the server and food cart, which was what she had secretly hoped would happen. It was the same man that brought their food last time. Paul assumed his position at the table, pen in hand, notebook in front of him. Kelley said, "Oh, do I get more help with my studies?" Shawna looked to see the waiters' reaction. He didn't look up from his duties lifting lids and setting things up for the group.

Paul spoke up and said, "Of course you do since we finished our books last night."

Shawna was relieved and grateful to him for doing that. When the waiter left, she walked over to Paul and said, "Thank you," and planted a sweet kiss right on his lips in front of Kelley. He kissed her back with a little too much passion. Kelley cleared her throat. They stopped kissing.

Kelley said, "Glad you volunteered to help. I can use another set of eyes." Shawna shook her head no. and at that Kelley stopped talking.

"What do you need help with?" asked Paul.

"Never mind. It's my responsibility. After all, I chose this topic of study. I just need to buckle down and get it done. Why don't you two go to your room Paul? I'll be right here when you get back."

"No. I won't be going to Paul's room today."

Paul said, "I think Kelley has a great idea. She needs this room to herself, needs the peace and quiet, and we could use my room to catch up."

Shawna said, "Maybe we could go for a walk."

"You guys could go to Tyler's for a drink," Kelley said.

"Beau needs some exercise, so if you want, we can walk him, maybe stop for a drink. I'm thinking I'd like hot cocoa instead of alcohol. I'm getting tired anyway." She yawned.

"Okay, sounds good. Kelley, you want us to bring you back anything?" he asked.

"No, thanks."

"See you soon," Shawna said as she clipped Beau's leash on him.

"Bye, guys, Kelley said. With Beau along, she felt she had an out for going back to Paul's room. Beau needed his meds soon and to sleep more. Truth be told, Beau would have slept in Paul's room if they would have gone back there, but she didn't want that. She wasn't going to do that to him. She would let him sleep through the night after his walk. Paul would have to understand.

As they walked and talked, her phone rang. It was Chandler. She was ecstatic to hear from him. Paul was put off by her enthusiasm when he heard another man's voice on the other end.

He wasn't eavesdropping. It was not hard to know who she was talking to when he could hear her part of the conversation. He heard her ask him when he was coming home. When she got off the phone, she explained her relationship with Chandler before Paul could ask her anything about him. He did ask if he was that guy that was coming into the restaurant that day he was leaving.

"What guy?"

"The one that looked like he had just stepped off of a photo shoot for G.Q. magazine."

"Ha ha, yeah, that's Chandler. He's more like a brother to me, though."

Paul said, "I can handle that. I'll just have to start dressing a little snappier." She laughed again and told him he had nothing to worry about. She didn't compare any man to Chandler. There was no comparison.

Chapter 34

They walked back to the hotel. Just outside the entrance, she saw creepy dead guy and a lot more spirits with him. They were looking around. She didn't know why but was sure it was for her. When they spotted her, they started walking toward her. Paul hadn't seen the zombie- like hoard approaching them. She grabbed Paul's hand and pulled him between the hotel and the building next door. They went in the hotel's fire exit. They got to her room and found Kelley on the balcony looking down and feeling very sick. All of the spirits in their death states was overwhelming to her. She looked green in the face. Paul asked her if she was going to be alright.

"Yeah, I just had a little too much to drink last night." Shawna knew why Kelley looked that way.

She said, "Come on Kelley, sit over here," gesturing toward Kelley's bed.

Paul said that he should go. Shawna thanked him for the hot cocoa and said she'd call him the next day. He patted Beau on the head and said, "See you, buddy." He left and went to his room.

Shawna said, "You saw them too, huh?"

"Yes. There are so many more of them now."

Shawna said, "I saw them when we came back from the coffee shop."

Kelley said, "But you don't feel their pain like I do. I felt them there before I went to see why I was feeling this way. Then, I saw all of them looking up here. Where are those Advils?" Shawna went to the nightstand and threw the bottle of pain relievers to Kelley. She took three. They talked about Kelley's theory as to why the spirits were hanging around and not crossing over further and puzzled over what they were going to do about it. Kelley said, "That one creepy dude didn't seem to want my help. You asked him what he wanted, and he didn't want to talk to you either."

"I hope they find resolution and leave us alone," Shawna said.

"Yeah, I don't think that's going to happen anytime soon. Why don't we just let them follow us when we check out of here and see what happens?" asked Kelley.

"I don't want them following me to my house. There's enough trouble there now."

"Again," Kelley said, "trust me, Shay!"

Shawna conceded and told Kelley about the call from Chandler and said, he'd be coming home no later than Sunday. "I couldn't talk Paul out of coming over this weekend, though."

"At least you'll have two men there, then."

"I suppose you're right," Shawna said.

"I usually am," Kelley said with a giggle.

Shawna said, "He wants to see where I live."

"I'll bet he does. He probably wants to checkout his competition, too. And I'm sure he wants to see all of you even more."

"And?" said Shawna.

Kelley smiled at her. Then she said, "Yeah, he's pretty cool."

"He is," Shawna said.

"It's good that he didn't try and push sex while he was here."

"No need," Shawna said.

"No?"

"Nope!"

"You naughty girl!" exclaimed Kelley.

"Yep!" Shawna said. "He can wait a couple more days now," she said.

"This is a side of you I've never seen, Shawna Marie! I like it!"

"Well, I have needs too!"

"How was it?"

"Kelley!"

"Oh, come on! Make with the details!"

"Well, if you were out on the deck of the catamaran instead of inside reading, you might have seen how he was."

"No! You did it at his house that day?"

"Yep."

"Okay, scale of one to ten."

"I don't know. I don't have any experience other than with Steele."

Kelley said, "He was hot too."

"He could be charming when he wanted to," Shawna said. "I guess I'd say I wouldn't kick Paul out of bed if, uh, when I get with him again."

"Alright, Shawna!" Shawna was surprised at Kelley's line of questioning and her reactions to Shawna's answers. "Kelley, are you a virgin?"

Kelley turned red. "No! Why would you ask that?"

"Because this is a conversation we'd be having in high school."

"Sorry, just making conversation. Trying to be cheeky."

"Huh, okay," Shawna said.

Just then, both girls' phones rang. Kelley said, "I'll ask her and get back to you. Okay, thanks."

Kelley was still on the phone, walking around and talking like she wanted privacy. Shawna was headed toward the bathroom. Kelley grabbed her arm, "What's your address?"

"Fifteen twenty-two South West Ridge Drive. Why?"

"Because I think we need an army to deal with what's at your house."

"But I don't want anyone going down in the basement until Chandler gets back. I don't want anyone near the house until then, period."

Kelley told the person on the other end that it would most likely be that coming Sunday and gave her the address. Then,

Shawna heard her saying, "Yes, it is an emergency, but yes, we have to wait until then. No, no one's there right now. Okay, thank you. We appreciate your help. See you then." She turned to Shawna and said, "We're all set for spiritual battle."

"Who was that?" asked Shawna.

"Raina. She's the High Priestess in my coven."

"Wow! Okay, I hope you know what you're doing," Shawna said.

"Trust me," Kelley said.

"Paul invited us to dinner tonight. Want to go?"

"That's nice of him. Sure, I'll go out with you guys, thanks. Where are we going?" asked Kelley.

"He said he'd leave it up to us."

"Cool. Maybe we can go to Tyler's place? I heard their prime rib rocks."

"I'll mention that to him," Shawna said. "We need to shop for clothes."

They went through the kitchen and out the back door waving to the chef, leaving Beau back in the room sleeping off his meds. They went to a boutique called All Dolled Up. They were pleasantly surprised by the variety of clothing. The store reminded them of a combination large chain store at the mall that sells jeans and a high- end vintage clothing store all in one. Kelley found a nice shirt and jacket to wear with jeans and boots. Shawna opted for a jumper. It was black with cutouts, sexy, but not too revealing. They both got jewelry to match, purses and shoes. Shawna found a cute peep toe pump and Kelley found the perfect pair of cool, chunky boots to complete her ensemble. They headed back to the hotel Kelley said, "Incoming!" Shawna looked and saw spirits coming from all directions. They surrounded the girls. Kelley addressed the creepy dead guy from the diner again. She asked him once again what he wanted from her.

"Nothing," he said.

"So, you do talk?"

He nodded.

She asked, "Why are you following us?" They all walked away from the girls instead of answering her question. "Huh," Kelley said. "Strange."

"Why didn't they say what they wanted?" asked Shawna.

"I don't know. It seems they wanted something. I may be a clairvoyant, but I'm no mind reader."

"What does *clairvoyant* mean, anyway?"

"It means *clear seeing*. You are one, too, now. I'm also clairaudient. You have that going on as well now. I have a lot of gifts in that area. My intuition is telling me to get back to my books. What time are we meeting Paul?"

"Eight."

"Well, that's not enough time. I'll hit it hard tomorrow. I've gotta tell you I saw your boy toy Chandler in the library one day reading a book. I followed him to where he returned it to the shelf and saw it was a book on how to make a Jacobs ladder."

"What's that?"

"It's a device that uses high voltage electricity. An electric spark bounces back and forth between two wires, then climbs up the ladder. It uses the air in between and takes the spark with it. There's an arc at the top when the electricity gets up there."

"And, what is the purpose of one of those things?"

"I don't know why he would be using one. He's not Dr. Frankenstein trying to revive a corpse. They're scientific novelty devices. Is he into that sort of thing?"

"Not that I know of."

"Well, I don't know why he'd be reading up on building one then. It was a month before he left for his trip when I saw him there."

"Yeah, that is strange. I'll have to ask him when I see him."

"No, don't. He'll think I was spying on him."

"Okay, I won't say anything then."

"Feel like going to the Candle Shoppe for a while?"

"I would, but I need to check on Beau before we meet Paul."

"Let's go do that then."

They did. Beau was fine, but since he was awake, they took him outside. They went for a walk for half an hour and they weren't alone. The spirits followed them into the hotel. Kelley said, "Give me Beau's leash. You go one way, and I'll take Beau to the room. Don't come to the room though. I'll meet you in the ladies' room with your clothes you're wearing to the restaurant."

"Why?"

"Because I think they're following you. This way, Beau won't get hurt or bothered while were gone."

She nodded. "I'll stay in the lobby while you take him upstairs." Beau turned around and looked at Shawna as Kelley led him off. Shawna said, "I'll see you soon, baby. Go to sleep until I get back." He seemed to understand because he willingly went away from her. She thought he just needed an encouraging word from her. The "I'll see you soon" is what she thought did it. That's what made her feel better, so she convinced herself of that. It wasn't like she'd be gone all night anyway. Sure enough, as soon as she was alone, they surrounded her. She should have known Kelley was right. Shawna was about to yell at them, but didn't want to look like a lunatic yelling for no reason in the lobby. She went into the bathroom as Kelley had told her to do in the first place. All of the spirits followed her in there. She couldn't believe how many had filed in after her. If they were alive, it would have been too crowded for everyone. Kelley told her once about our molecular structure's being denser than a spirit's and that a hundred of them could easily fit into a small space like an elevator or in this case a women's restroom. Shawna was to the point of fuming when she asked, "Why are you all following me?"

The creepy dead guy stepped forward and said, "You should know by now. We can't just tell you. Don't you realize you are needed?"

She answered, "If I knew how to help you all, I would! Now, I'm leaving soon and you are not allowed to follow me. I'll talk with my friend and figure out how I can help you. I'm sorry I don't know what it is that you need from me now, but she'll help me figure it out. I have to go now." The spirits followed her out to the lobby and all waited there for her to figure out what was needed.

Kelley came downstairs and when the elevator doors opened, she was floored by the number of "ghosties" in the lobby. Shawna said, "I know. Let's go wait outside. I told them they couldn't follow us anymore."

Kelley said, "Thank goodness. I wouldn't be able to eat if they were around."

"You were right, Kel. They do want something from me."

"I knew it."

"Then share, please."

"Well, that's just it. I don't know what it is that they want, but I know it has to do with you and your crystal." Paul pulled up just then. Kelley said, "We'll talk more later tonight about it all."

Chapter 35

Chandler and Conor headed to Edinburgh Castle. Supposedly, the relic is on display there with The Honours of Scotland, a crown, scepter and a sword placed on either side of the Stone of Jacob. Chandler wondered if they were forgeries and not the actual relic and Honours. The Stone had been stolen before, and he wouldn't have been surprised if they displayed the forgeries and had the real ones put away for safe keeping. The only way to know was to get up close and personal with it, and that's what he intended to do. There were a lot of people there and just as many demons. He had Conor call the local Knights Templar. He thought they would create a distraction, so he'd be able to get a piece of the Stone after examining it. The men were on their way.

Chandler followed a group of tourists into the room where the Stone was kept. He walked close to the display, and read what the placard said about the Stone. It read; Jacob's pillow, also known as Jacob's Stone is said to have mystical powers. Jacob from the Bible fell asleep under the stars on the Stone, therefore the name Jacob's Pillow. He dreamed of a ladder to Heaven while sleeping on the Stone one night. Thus, the term Jacob's ladder for a machine with electrically charged currents that arc at the top of two parallel wires that repel each other. The sparks heat up the air and the hot air rises, creating an arc at the top of the tube they originated from. It is also known as The Coronation Stone as Kings and Queens have sat on the throne with The Stone of Jacob placed underneath the throne and have been sworn into their positions as royalty. It is also known as The Tanist Stone and The Stone of Scone. It was dubbed The Tanist Stone as Kings and Queens of Scotland would be crowned above it as the English did. The English called Jacob's Pillow The Stone of Scone (Stone of Scoon) in English.

 The exhibit was guarded by two armed men on either side of the display. That answered his question about forgeries. Conor's brothers in the Order showed up. They immediately recognized the evil ones there. They had brought Holy water, crucifixes, sage and sweet grass with them. Promptly, they lit the sage and sweet grass to fog it up in there. They had visited the castle the night before posing as tourists and saw there were eight cameras on the main floor and four exits, so eight of the men went by each of the cameras and lit the bundles. Most of the Knights surrounded the demons and threw Holy water on them. Chandler charmed the staff so they fell into a deep sleep. He could have just done that in England, but he couldn't resist the idea of them chasing their horses around. It may have been more challenging for him, but it was worth it. Conor lit sage and sweet grass by the fire alarm next to the display. In doing so, the alarm made the humans evacuate the building.

Conor had snuck onto the grounds the night before when the exhibit was closed and filled the waters holding tank with Holy water that was blessed by the Pope himself, so when it rained water out of the buildings automatic sprinkler system, it was like acid to the evil ones. They screeched and screamed in pain. Chandler was able to pry open the part of The Jacob's Stone that had been replaced after someone put a scroll in it. That was documented in a newspaper article he had read a decade earlier. He grabbed a piece of the Stone from inside there and replaced the missing piece. The Stone had been stolen by three college or high school students one time. He thinks that happened in Ireland. He wasn't sure of their level of education. He didn't know who put the scroll in the Stone either, or what was written on it, but he didn't need to know. He got what he came for. The Stone and The Honours of Scotland were still in the display case. The guards would wake up a minute after he and The Knights Templar left to protect the precious items and that's all that mattered. He snapped his fingers when he got to the gate and the guards woke up. All of them were looking around to see if their fellow guards had seen them sleeping on the job, and all running around soaking wet wondering where the fire had originated that made the water spray down from the ceiling and soak them all.

Chandler's job there was done. Now, the third and most important job awaited him back home. He secured the next available flight back to the States. It would be in the morning. Conor invited him to a local pub with the brothers in the Order. The men were more than excited to formally meet this latest resident from The Other Side, and their prior first leader in their Order. The Knights Templar were a brave group of men. They were established two centuries ago. They were known then as Pauperes commilitones Christi Templique Solominici. (The poor fellow soldiers of Christ). These men dedicated their lives to Christ. They knew what they were getting into when they signed up. Their agenda was to defend all from evil. They did a great job helping Chandler at the castle. They would be able to help back home. He was sure of that. This particular group of knights didn't need to accompany him back to the States. There were chapters of the Order all over. He was certain Conor knew men all over the world with the same agenda and some would be near Spring Lake.

"Conor, you want to see this through to the end?"

Conor smiled and said, "That's my job."

Chandler said, "Good. The plane leaves at six a.m. Do you have a passport?"

"Sure do."

Chapter 36

The girls were in the lobby waiting for Paul to drive around front and pick them up. They had all agreed on Tyler's restaurant for dinner. They all had the prime rib and shrimp. Tyler brought out a bottle of Merlot. He sat with them and talked, having the trio sample the shrimp Dijon, stuffed crab rolls and lobster lasagna for appetizers. When their meals arrived, he poured the Merlot and left them to enjoy their dinners.

Shawna said, "I miss Jess and Gussy."

"Who are they?" asked Paul.

"My next-door neighbor and his dog."

"We'll go by and see them in the morning," Kelley said. "We need to get some sleep tonight."

"Yeah, he's most likely asleep now," Shawna said.

"How old is he?" asked Paul.

"I don't know. I'd guess him at eighty," Shawna said. "I miss my house, too."

Kelley said, "It's time to pack up and go home anyway."

"Chandler called again. The call was staticky. I heard him say he was coming home tomorrow for sure though."

Kelley said, "Good, then plans will stay the same."

Paul was distracted by the dessert cart and called the guy over. "Anything catch your eye, girls?"

"No, none for me, thanks," Shawna said.

"Yeah, I'm stuffed, too." Kelley held her hand over her stomach.

Paul got a piece of cherry pie to go and drove the girls back to the hotel. The spooks followed them. This time they saw where their room was. Shawna told them they had to stay out of the room.

When they walked into their room, there was a maid in there. Kelley said, "What are you doing here?"

She answered, "I'm here for Mrs. Claire Dumont."

At that moment, a woman stormed out of the bathroom ranting about her jewelry and bubble bath she couldn't find. "And where is my dress I'm supposed to wear tonight, Maria? Why can't I find my things?"

Shawna said, "You're in the wrong room!"

At that, the woman became irate. She said, "This is my room! Just who do you think you are, young lady? And what are you doing in my room?! My husband Arthur rented this room for me a week ago!" Kelley thought that he most likely did that so he could be out with his paramour or in the girls' room. Shawna looked at Kelley. Kelley shook her head and walked into the bathroom. She saw a bloody scene in there as if out of a horror movie. She peered around the corner out into the main area of the suite at the maid Maria and saw she had a gunshot wound right between her eyes. It appeared Mrs. Dumont had been murdered in the bathroom. It also appeared the woman was dressed from the nineteen-thirties. Maria's uniform was outdated, too.

Kelley saw the scene play out in her head. She whispered to Shawna, "The husband killed his wife. He took her jewelry to make it look like a robbery. The maid had been gunned down when she ran to help her employer." Then loudly, she said, "We're sorry. We must be mistaken. Perhaps our reservations are for next week." Shawna protested, but Kelley shook her head again. "Let's pack our things and go now, Shay." She had Shawna get the stuff from the bathroom. She didn't want to see brains splattered all over the wall, a bathtub with a naked woman in it full of blood, or the maid's body lying there again. Shawna went and got their stuff out of there. She wouldn't see any of it, so it wasn't unfair to ask her to go in their sparkling clean bathroom that the maid service just cleaned and get their things.

Kelley piled the books up on the table, notebooks, too, and grabbed their suitcases. Shawna called down for a cart to take their belongings downstairs. Mrs. Dumont had been griping the whole time. Now, she was yelling into the phone. Shawna didn't pay any attention to her after she heard from Kelley that they were disembodied spirits. Shawna picked up Beau and got him off the bed, put his leash on, and answered the door for the bellhop. That

Dumont woman was ranting and raving about a dog being in *her* room, and she was furious with the man that came to the door to help the girls leave. The last thing they heard from her before the door was shut was, "I'll have your job for this!"

Chapter 37

Kelley explained everything to Shawna in front of the man that came to help them to their car. Shawna said, "I can't believe she kept her mouth shut for as long as she had while we stayed there." Shawna also said how sorry she was for Kelley having to see all of that when all she saw was two women in her room like anyone else she'd see on the street.

"I'm used to it."

"I hope *she* doesn't follow us home too."

Kelley said, "She won't. Some spirits are so attached to their personas, their earthly goods, and to this plain that they linger for hundreds of years, decades, or however long it takes them to cross over. To them, time stands still."

"Hopefully they aren't reliving that horrible, bloody night over and over again, though."

Kelley looked at Karl and saw the look of bewilderment on his face. She said, "She's helping me with a part I have in a play."

He said, "Sounds like a good one."

Down in the lobby, the horde of zombie like spirits were waiting for the girls. "I knew it!" Kelley said. "They're following you because of that crystal. Are you sure you want to keep it?"

"They can't have my crystal. Do you think it was that gross woman's in the parking lot? Or creepy dead guy's?"

"They don't want the crystal. They're following you because you have it, though. I'm wondering if it will open a portal, something like that."

"I don't know how to do that, and even if I did, that's dangerous! You never want to do that! You don't know who or what will come from it!"

"That's right. Glad you've been paying attention in class."

Shawna said, "That's not just in Theology. It's common sense just like the bad things that can come from using a Ouija board."

"Yes, I know. I'll never live that one down."

"Well look what's been happening since we used it!"

"Shawna. You had an issue prior to my bringing the board into your house, and you also started seeing spirits before I even came over that day. You've seen them since you were a kid. Besides, we didn't use the board! Remember? We didn't ask it any questions. The only thing we did was touch that board, and that was after I saged the shit out of it."

"Yeah, I know you did. I'm sorry."

"Don't be. I know you're just freaking out, but don't worry. I have a feeling when we get back to your place and Hottie's there, things will be clearer, and you'll feel a lot better."

"I hope so," Shawna said.

They got their things loaded into Shawna's car and left for her house. When they got there all was quiet from their vantage point in the car. Shawna went over to Jess' house and knocked. Kelley stayed in the car. A man Shawna didn't recognize answered the door He had a realtor's blazer on. "Who are you? And, where's Jess?"

"Jess who?" he asked.

"My neighbor Jess!"

"I don't know any Jess, Ma'am. I'm Nicholas Swan, from Swan and Associate's Realtors."

"Why are you here?"

"I'm here to sell this house. "

"My friend lives here and you shouldn't be here!"

"This house has been empty for decades, ma'am." Shawna just stared at him in shock. A couple were poking around in Jess' house too. That set her off and made her even angrier.

"This is my friend's house! He must be on vacation. He has a beautiful garden outside. He keeps it very nice. He works in it every night!"

"Ma'am, no one has lived here since before I was born. You're mistaken."

"Just look at his garden—"

As she ran outside to make her point, she was shocked when she saw nearly four feet of overgrown grass in back, weeds where a garden used to be, and Jess' rocker dilapidated on its side, and a dry cracked bowl that was Gussy's water bowl broken in half. She ran inside, and looked for his things, opening cupboards and closets. She had to find a sign that he and his precious Gussy did in fact live next door to her. There was nothing, not a stitch of clothing, not a remnant of him or her to prove their existence or that they had *ever* lived there. The man said, "Are you okay?"

Kelley walked up. She looked sad and dropped her head.

Shawna said to the man, "This isn't over! I'll be back with the owner of this home! You people will be in big trouble!" She, Kelley and Beau walked away. Shawna stopped Kelley by her arm. "What do you know?"

Kelley looked as if she were holding back tears with her lips pursed. Then, she looked behind Shawna and her expression changed. Kelley said, "I'll let him tell you himself." Shawna turned to see what Kelley meant. There stood Jess, Gussy at his side. She ran to Jess and hugged him, saying, "Oh, Jess, I was so worried about you two." She pulled back from his embrace to ask him questions and that's when she noticed the gash on his forehead. "What happened to you?"

Jess said, "We've been gone a long time, Missy." She looked at Gussy, and she looked perfectly healthy. He said, "Oh, Gussy went in her sleep of natural causes. Me? I fell and hit my head on that fireplace of yours, Missy."

"But, why? Why don't you cross over?"

"My wife won't leave without her brother, and I'm waiting for her."

Kelley handed Shawna an old newspaper clipping and said, "I did some research." It was an obituary. It read,

> "Friday, June twelve, Eighteen seventy- four. Jessup Athy Stickler, age Eighty-four was found dead in his home from a wound to the head. Upon further investigation, it was determined that his death was accidental."

With all her knowledge of the afterlife, Shawna was still so sad to know her friend wasn't alive even though he was standing right in front of her talking to her.

Chapter 38

Just then, Chandler walked up with Conor. He made the introductions to the girls. As he turned to introduce him, Jess and Gussy vanished. Chandler didn't look surprised. Conor hadn't seen them at all. That ticked Shawna off. She pulled Chandler to the side and said, "How long have you known?" Before he could attempt to answer she added, "What else have you kept from me?"

He said, "We do need to talk."

"You're damn right we do! Are you a clairvoyant like Kelley?"

"No, hon, I'm not."

"Don't talk down to me, Chandler!"

"I'm not, Shawna. I love you."

"Then why aren't you honest with me?"

"I have been honest. Everything I've ever said to you is the God's honest truth!"

"And what aren't you telling me?" she asked.

"There's where you have me. I have a lot to tell you, but I haven't been able to until now, until you were ready."

"Ready for what?"

"We need to go sit down and talk calmly."

"In my house with whatever's in there?"

"Yes, in there, but you'll—we'll—be protected."

"How?"

"With prayers of protection and lots of support. Conor knows what's going on too."

"So, you told him before me? Who else knows?"

"A lot of people. And you should too by now."

"What do you mean?"

"Don't you feel it?" She had her crystal in her hand rolling it inside her sweatshirt pocket when he asked her that. She didn't answer him. "Can't you tell that you were made for something special? You have a higher purpose. I was hoping you'd come to realize on your own since I left that Selenite crystal for you."

"It's yours?"

"No, it was meant for you. Do you feel you have to take it everywhere with you?"

She said, "Yes."

"Then you feel the connection."

"Yeah, and I don't know why, but I know I want it with me all the time, even when I shower. Why is that?" she asked.

Chandler answered, "It's natural for that to happen when you're the one meant for the crystal."

221

"Could you stop being so vague and explain this attachment I have to a rock, please?"

"Let's go over to your house, sit down, and you have some wine, and we'll talk."

"Now I'm nervous. Come on, Kelley. Let's go to my house and talk with Chandler." Chandler and Shawna walked to her house, Conor and Kelley trailing behind. Kelley didn't think there would be another guy anywhere near as alluring as Chandler was, but she was attracted to this man. She even asked him if he owned a kilt. Shawna overheard that and called Kelley a shameless flirt. Kelley answered, "And?" Shawna wondered if Kelley knew the meaning of the word "tact." *Yeah, not subtle at all*, thought Shawna.

They got to the threshold of her house and all of the sudden, all the banging and smashing of furniture started. They knew they were dealing with an intelligent entity. It seemed it was planning its next move. Up from behind them on the sidewalk came Shawna's professor, the nun, and the rabbi who were in class one day seeming to be looking for someone but didn't address the students then. "Professor? What are you doing here?" asked Shawna.

He answered, "We're here to help, Ms. Livingston. This is Father Guillermo Martinez and Sister Anna Maria Sanchez. They will help you with your "problem.''

Shawna looked sideways at Kelley.

"I called them," Kelley said.

''Please go on in. We'll be right behind you," said Shawna.

"I'm afraid I must take my leave now," said the professor.

"Thank you for coming, Professor."

"Yes, thank you," said Kelley.

"Of course, ladies. My pleasure to help."

The priest and nun entered, and a huge roar, followed by a menacing growl, echoed throughout the house. They didn't need to be told where to go. The nun followed the priest toward the basement, clutching her rosary beads.

After them came twelve of the Knights Templar in the local order of the chapter. Kelley swooned.

They all entered the house and headed for the basement, except Chandler, Shawna, and Kelley. He got the girls each a glass of wine, sat down on the living room couch and held Shawna's hand. He said, "What I'm about to tell you is a lot for you to understand. Let me speak, and then you can ask your questions. Okay?" She nodded. "I knew your great-great-grandparents and ancestors before them."

"I'm supposed to believe you're a few hundred years old? Here we go!"

Kelley said, "Let him talk."

"Sorry," Shawna said.

"Thank you," Chandler said. "I've been around longer than that. Actually, I'm from the Tribe of Dan (Towatha de Denan). I've been a Celt, too."

Kelley couldn't resist. "Do you own a kilt, Chandler?"

He ignored that question. He knew it was rhetoric, to be funny and flirt with him. "You were here before. We knew each other back then. You just don't remember. You only have your memories here, now in this flesh body."

Shawna opened her mouth to speak. Kelley shushed her and said, "I believe him, Shawna."

He continued talking. "You have a secret in your ancestry, Shawna. You are a very distant relative of Jacob from the Bible."

"Whoa!" Kelley said. She was listening intently, hanging on his every word.

Shawna coughed up her wine. "Do you really expect me to believe that? Really?"

"You agreed to listen and not speak until I was done talking. And yes, I expect you to believe everything I'm saying. I would never lie to you."

"Maybe not, but you haven't told me the truth about everything, and you've kept things from me."

"Yes, to protect you, and for you to realize your destiny on your own. I'm your spirit guide, Shawna."

"I knew it!" exclaimed Kelley.

"My spirit guide? Hmm, what are you guiding me toward?" she asked cynically.

"At this point, you should have some idea," Chandler said.

"Oooh, I know!" yelled Kelley.

"And what do you know, Kelley?" he asked.

"I know it has something to do with helping spirits and the crystal she has because they've been following her around since she's had it."

"Very good, Kelley. Come here."

"Me?" Kelley asked.

"Yes, you." She sat next to him and he put his arm around her and fingered through her hair to tease her. "You're a natural blond?"

"Very funny," Kelley said.

Shawna laughed and said, "I thought it was."

Kelley said, "Yes, I'm a blond, and I'm very smart."

"Yes, you are, and very unique," Chandler said.

"Because I'm smart and blond?"

"No, because you are you," Chandler said. "You suffer and don't let others know of your pain."

Shawna looked perplexed. Kelley quickly changed the subject. "Let's talk about Shawna's destiny."

"What pain?" asked Shawna.

Chandler said nothing but waited for Kelley to tell her best friend. "I'm fine, Shay. Don't worry about me."

Shawna said, "Nothing was broken, was it?"

"No."

"You should have gone to the hospital the other night."

"You know I don't like hospitals or doctor visits. I'm fine, Shawna."

"You're sure?"

"Yes, I'm sure. Stop worrying so much."

"If you say so." Shawna dropped the subject, hoping Chandler was talking about Kelley's getting thrown around the other day.

They heard a loud roar coming from the basement. Chandler said, "The Knights are doing their job." He got up and headed downstairs with a lot of Shawna's questions left unanswered.

The girls followed him. Beau tagged along. The questions wouldn't stay unanswered for long. She got mad and yelled his name. "Chandler!" He turned toward her. "Tell me what I need to know now!"

Chapter 39

"Here? Now?" Chandler asked.

"Yes, now."

"In front of everyone?"

"Why not? They all seem to know a lot more about what's going on than me."

"Shawna, I was trying to protect you. I told you I had hoped you'd figure it out yourself. I didn't want to upset you."

"Well. I'm beyond that now, so tell me, please."

He inhaled deeply and began, "As I told you, I've been around your ancestors, and every one of them have been given the crystal, and none of them have had an attachment to it like you do. It's you, Shawna. You are the one I've waited for."

"Waited for what?"

"You are the one who will cross over lost souls and bring them peace. The Dilatory, the curtain raiser. You'll lift the veil so lost souls can cross over to the Other Side."

"What?"

"It's your destiny."

"What if I don't want that responsibility?"

"Then that's your choice. You have free will. God gave us all free will. That's why there's evil in the world. When your great-great-grandfather found he couldn't help and the time was coming close, he sacrificed himself, and locked himself behind that leaded door with the demon that came to snatch the souls before they could cross over."

"You're mistaken."

"No, Shawna. I'm not."

"He passed away on a trip to Maltese."

"That's what you were told. Now, I don't know if that thing's here out of allegiance to the main evil one, or if it's trying to take the reins itself, but that's what's behind that door there." He had said that pointing to the huge leaded door.

"Are you kidding me? Why would something like that be here, and in my house?"

"It's here because it knew spirits would come to you or one of your relatives for help because of your lineage. It's not alone, either. There are more of them here."

"Then I have no choice but to get rid of them," Shawna said.

"That's why everyone came. We're going to help you with that."

There was a knock at the front door. "That's probably Raina," Kelley said.

"Or Paul," Shawna said. I asked him to come. Chandler gave her a quizzical look. "He's an old friend. Remember the guy from The Robin's Nest?"

"Ah."

"I've wanted you to meet him, but not like this with all of this going on here." Shawna and Chandler went upstairs. The Knights split up. Half of them went upstairs too. It was both Paul and Raina at the door. "Paul, this is my, uh, Chandler. This is my uh, Paul. The men shook hands.

"Everyone, this is Raina. She's the High Priestess in my coven," Kelley said.

"Hi, Raina. Thanks for coming," Shawna said.

"Where is this son of a bitch?" asked Raina.

On cue, it screamed so loudly it rattled the windows. Then, they heard, "Kellllleeeeeey, Kelllleeeeeey," called from the upstairs landing.

Kelley said, "Nana?" An old lady, complete with the shawl over her shoulders, pinafore on and orthotic shoes started down the stairs. She had a cat in her hands. "Fidget!" exclaimed Kelley.

"No, Kelley! That's not your grandmother or your cat," Chandler said, grabbing her arm to stop her from running up the stairs. She shook his arm off and ran up there.

Raina stopped Chandler from going after her. She shook her head and quietly said, "She knows what she's doing."

"I've brought Fidget for you," said the old lady.

Kelley reached into her bag on her hip and pulled something out, saying, "I've got something for you, too, Nana. I saved it for when you'd come to me."

The old lady smiled and said, "How nice, Dear."

In one fell swoop, Kelley pulled out a sachet of sweet grass and sage, lit it, and crammed it in the old lady's mouth. She gagged on it, spit it out, and screeched. She dropped the cat that turned into the skeletal remains of a nearby once-buried cat that had already been desiccated. Once it hit the floor, the remains turned to dust. The thing screamed, "You bitch!" and knocked Kelley upside her head. The blow sent her flying down the stairs. Conor was on the second floor and heard the thing's screech and the sound of Kelley tumbling down the stairs. He came up from behind the thing and decapitated the "old woman" with his sword that had been soaked in holy water, seeing right through the façade. The head rolled down on Kelley at the stair landing. She shuddered and threw it off of her. Paul jumped as the head was thrown in their direction near the front door. "Damn," said Paul. He pulled Shawna close to him and held her there. "I warned you about what was happening here." Shawna said. He nodded, raised his eyebrows and exaggeratedly wiped his brow.

The demon then raised its hand, gestured toward Conor, flicked its bony wrist in the air as if shaking off something from it, and sent Conor sailing through the air, crashing into a wall behind him. Still standing, the creature's headless body started to wriggle as if full of worms. Out from the neck came a demon's head in short, jerking movements, left, right, left, until the whole ugly, evil face emerged. It cackled, and then said to Kelley, with its own voice, a deep resonating baritone, "What's the matter, deary? Don't you want to kiss your Nana?" A steely V-shaped tongue shot out of its mouth ten feet from where it stood at the top of the steps and swiped a slimy, stinking lick across Kelley's nose and mouth. Then, it went down her chest to her crotch as she lay there at the bottom of the stairs. It slurped its tongue back into its mouth. It said, "I smell it," laughing more. She spit after that, ran toward it, the others following closely behind her, Chandler running past them all. Conor beat them to it. He came up from behind it and poured a bucket of Holy water on it. The creature howled in pain and melted into a pile of clothing, leaving a stinking, rotted, steaming, sulfur-smelling pile of wet material where it had been.

There was an evil screech from the basement. They all ran down there and found the others performing their religious rituals all at once. "Nihil (No)!" yelled the demon behind the thickly leaded door.

The priest repeated his words, "Give me your name!"

"Raaaaaaaaaargh!" came from behind the door, then a gravelly laugh.

"Sanctus, Dominus, Saboath (Holy, Holy, Holy. Lord God of Host)," said the priest. He and the nun took communion there.

"Nihil (No)!" said the creature.

"Nefaruim rem operati estis mala (You evil, wicked thing)," said the priest.

"Consuetudo est Magna virtus (Great is the power of habit)," said the Rabbi, rocking back and forth as he performed his ritual.

Upstairs, another knock on the front door drew their attention. Chandler said, "I'll get it." A few men in the order went with him for safety's sake. It was the Shinto Monk he had asked to come. By the noises coming from the basement, he didn't need to be told where to go. He threw salt over his shoulder before crossing the threshold into the house per his religions rituals. They do that so no demons follow them. He carried a tall stick with long strands of cloth tied at the top of it. He wore his ceremonial cap and robe. Chandler thanked him for coming. He nodded. He headed straight downstairs leaving a trail of salt in his wake. Chandler followed him down. When they got to the basement, Chandler went to the furnace room, and pulled out the Jacob's ladder he had made before his trip. He started it up.

As everyone was performing his or her own ritual, Kelley said to Chandler, "I knew there was a reason you were reading that book at the library"

"You saw me?"

"You're hard to miss."

He said, "This is a Jacob's Ladder. It's based on a dream Jacob from the Bible had when he slept on the stone and dreamed of a ladder to Heaven. The Stone is known as Jacob's Pillow, Jacob's Stone, the Coronation Stone, the Tanist Stone. It has a couple more names. The point is, we can use this as a means of tormenting that thing behind the door since it's named after a relic with religious origins."

Chandler put the Jacob's ladder right outside the door that imprisoned the demon. It buzzed, and as the current reached the top of the unit, it arced its electricity.

It annoyed the demon. That was apparent as the Jacob's ladder slid fifteen feet from its original spot in front of the door, seemingly of its own accord and crashed into the wall on the other side of the basement.

It did agitate the creature as Chandler had planned, but he had hoped its presence there would have made a greater impact.

Chapter 40

Chandler pulled Shawna aside and said, "You're owed your explanation."

"You think?"

"Don't be angry with me, Shawna. I'm sorry that we didn't have our privacy I think you need to make your decision. You need to know that you will be leading those souls into the light, not just lifting the veil."

"I'm not going anywhere without Beau, so find someone else to do it. I am not taking away any time he'd have here to live."

"Seriously, Shawna? Life here is nothing compared to life over there. You both will be forever young, happy, and healthy. Why would you want him to stay here alone and die of old age? And you know he would never want to be without you."

"When you put it that way, I'm happy to go if it means he will live forever and I can have him with me."

"Don't worry about that. And you're not ending his life here. You're merely taking him Home to live forever together. No death, no sadness or anger. Those emotions do not exist where God's love fills the very air we breathe."

"What about my parents? My brother Kriss? Do they know? Your parents will explain it all when he leaves College in Florida. He'll inherit this house in a few years." Shawna nodded. "He is my brother. He'll want to know where I am when he comes to visit in the summer."

"Your parents know what to say."

Without another word, Shawna pulled her cell phone from her pocket and dialed her mother. "Mom, it's me."

"I know, honey."

"I love you."

"I love you, too, so very much sweetheart. If I could do it for you, I would."

"I know, Mom. Just think of it as a trip away for me, like this trip we all made here. I'll see you soon. Bye—no. See you later."

"Love you, honey." Her mom hung up crying.

Shawna took the piece of the relic from Chandler and she said, "I have to go find Kelley and talk to her." She found her dressing in her ceremonial Wiccan dress. It was white and looked similar to a toga. Shawna told her everything. They hugged.

Kelley said, "I've got to go downstairs and help Raina."

Shawna said, "I've got to pee really quick." Beau went in the bathroom with her as usual.

Kelley got to the living room and the doorbell rang. No one was there when she opened the door. The priest had come upstairs. When Kelley turned around, she was face to face with him. "How can I help you, Father?" He dropped to the floor. Kelley tried to help him up. He became rigid, stiff as a board. The man looked as if he weighed one-hundred thirty, maybe forty at best. To her, he felt five times that weight. She reached in his breast pockets to see if there was some medicine he might need. She was looking for nitro glycerin. She found nothing. She checked his pants pockets. Nothing there either. As she tried to pick him up, he grabbed both of her wrists. Then a deep guttural laugh came out of him.

Shawna had started downstairs after using the bathroom and saw Kelley trying to help the man up. The priest pulled Kelley down on him. Beau ran down the stairs ahead of Shawna. He barked and barked, advancing on them, then backing up. Shawna ran down after him and held her stone against the priest's forehead. It started smoking and burned a hole in the man's head. She knew it wasn't the priest then. She pulled her hand back with the stone in it. Kelley jumped up away from him. The priest morphed into a two-headed creature with a similar replica of Kelley's head on its shoulder, four arms, and four legs protruding from its trunk. It had a pair of women's breasts on one side of it. It was in a position where it looked like a man and woman having sex, but it was one body. Raina had come upstairs from the basement, her sixth sense leading her, telling her something was wrong. She saw the scene in the living room. She ran up and poured Holy water on the creature. It screamed in pain. She dropped a crucifix in the hole that Shawna had burned in its "head" and the forehead melted into slimy, viscous fluid on the floor, exposing the inside of the head, which was an empty shell. The "body" disintegrated one section at a time into liquid, writhing violently until nothing was left but part of the head, then the mouth and an eye. The tongue had hung out as a strangling noise came from what was left of the throat. The eye popped, fluid flew from it, hit a lamp in the living room and burned a hole in the shade. The clothes except the collar were burned away. Kelley should have known it wasn't the priest. It didn't wear a crucifix. What was left of the trunk of the creature sunk into the floor leaving only a priest's collar and the crucifix where it had been and a steaming pile of acrid fluid. Kelley poured Holy water on that and it all disappeared into the floor with a sizzle except the cross.

Concerned, Chandler, Conor, and some of the Knights Templar and the priest ran upstairs when they heard all the commotion and the girls and Beau were not with them, leaving the others down in the basement to continue their rituals in their attempt to weaken the demon behind the leaded door.

By that time, only Raina and Kelley were in the living room. Beau and Shawna, it seemed were nowhere to be found. "Where's Shawna?" asked Chandler.

"She was just here." They heard Beau barking upstairs. Everyone ran upstairs, looking for Shawna. They found Beau at the threshold of Shawna's bedroom. They looked in there and saw Shawna nude, standing by her bed. The men looked away. She said, "Chand, I can't find my stone. Come to me." She held her arms out. Chandler lifted his head and looked. "You know you want me," she said.

"I want you. Until I found the stone, I didn't realize how much I wanted you." She sat on the edge of her bed, spread her legs, and stuck her finger in herself. Then she rubbed it on her nose and mouth and licked her finger. Chandler hurried over to her. He got above her, lying over her. She went right for his belt.

Shawna and Paul came upon the scene. Beau barked his happy bark, seeing his mistress. "I'm sorry, baby." Chandler quickly turned his head to see Shawna and Paul standing there. She was embarrassed beyond words at what she saw. Shawna was mortified at the thing having taken her shape right down to the mole on her hip, and the way she grooms herself. She turned beet red and ran off, Beau and Paul following her. Chandler raised a sword he had pulled from a nearby Knights scabbard and drove it down on the head, slicing through the body cutting it in half. He knew his Shawna would not be that vulgar, not to mention Beau didn't want to get anywhere near this version of her. Beau knew it wasn't his mistress. He would never be fooled by an imposter. She was modest.

Out from what was left of the body came, "Meretrix illa cogitasti et (You thought I was that whore)." A deep menacing laugh followed. "Heh, heh heh." He dumped Holy water on it. It screamed, "Eo enim flagrante (It burns)!"

"Good," Chandler said, and it melted away.

Chandler called for Shawna. She came running, Beau at her heels, Paul close behind. She ran into Chandler's arms and cried. She had been embarrassed to tears. "I knew it wasn't you, Honey," he said.

"Where's Kelley?"

"In the bathroom, I think," Shawna said between sobs.

"Don't separate anymore unless, of course, you have to use the toilet, but stand outside when one of you goes in there. Don't women go in there together anyway?" Chandler asked.

"It depends on why we go in there," Shawna said wiping her eyes. They went to the bathroom door and heard Kelley vomiting, then the toilet flushing. Shawna knocked and said, "Are you alright in there, Kelley?"

Kelley opened the door, walked back to the sink, rinsed her mouth out, and washed her face. She could not have cared less that Chandler was standing right there, watching. She answered, "I've been better." Chandler went into the bathroom and put his arms around Kelley and led her out of there. She said, "I ought to get sick more often."

Chandler said, "No, we don't want you sick, Kelley. Are you well enough to participate with us in the basement?"

"Try and keep me away," Kelley said. He laughed. They all went back downstairs. Shawna had her crystal and the piece of Jacob's Stone with her.

Chapter 41

Everyone gathered down in the basement. Kelley joined Raina in her ritual, with Kelley repeating the mantra "good always wins over evil." The Shinto monk had surrounded everyone in a circle of salt except Paul. He stayed on the basement stairs and watched it all. The monk walked over to Paul throwing salt over his shoulder and encircled Paul in salt to protect him too telling him to not step out of that circle. They figured they had most of the main religions covered, enough to do battle against darkness. They had Christianity, Catholicism, Judaism, and the religion of the monk, and of course, Kelley and Raina's Wicca. That is a more widely spread religion than a lot of people thought and still think, so they had their bases covered.

No matter what their differences in their belief systems and traditions, rites, and rituals, they all believed in a higher power, and that is God, and that's what mattered.

"Be gone unclean spirit, along with every satanic power!" yelled the priest. The demon roared and a chair flew at the priest, just missed his head, and hit Kelley. She flew with it and hit the basement's concrete wall. She got up crying with a broken clavicle, sore neck and head, bruised ribs, and a painful leg. The right side of her body had hit the wall underneath the heavy Gothic chair that was part of Shawna's Great grandparents' set that was stored down in the basement. Shawna and Chandler ran to her side. She tried to hide her tears, but when Chandler grabbed her, and hugged her putting her head on his shoulder, they flowed in torrents. There was so much on her mind, yet she set it all aside, didn't want to admit that she was sick. No! This isn't possible! She didn't do anything to deserve this! The demon cackled when it heard her crying. She stopped crying, shoved off of Chandler's chest, picked up her sage and sweet grass bundle, and threw it right in front of the door that imprisoned the evil creature.

She said, "Suck on this!" The creature screamed with disdain. She laughed at that between hiccupping her sobs. It hurt her to hold the bundle, but she managed. Her right hand wasn't her dominant one, so she lucked out there. She was able to do the majority of things, lighting the lighter, and throwing the bundle with her left hand even though she had just had an operation on that hand. She was proud of herself for that, for everything, but it sure hurt throwing it and Hottie moving her head and hugging her hurt, but she wasn't about to complain about getting that close to him. She could hardly hold her head up and he bent it for her to rest it on his shoulder not knowing there was a broken bone attached to it! She figured if that monster killed her, she'd go Home with no regrets, but one, not letting Hottie have her virginity. She couldn't throw it at him anymore than she had with the exception of getting buck naked and begging him. She was about ready to just come out and ask him for sex, especially after he held her like that.

Well, at least he saw what she had underneath her dress. She hadn't put panties on. With her Wiccan dress, she never wore them. It was part of her feeling free, one with nature. Problem was everyone else saw, too. She was mortified by that! She was in love with him, but no one knew, not even Shawna. Shawna wouldn't make fun of her for being a virgin in love with an ethereal being. She's her best friend. She loves her. She'd be cool about it, but still Kelley was embarrassed by her purity, which in this day and age is very admirable, but she'd rather not admit that all she'd done was kiss one dude when she was twenty. The jerk put his hand down her pants. She wanted to kick his ass. By the time she was done screaming at him, he was backing up with his hands in the air, calling her a cock tease and a crazy bitch. She hardly knew the idiot. *One kiss does not entitle a guy to all of her,* she thought. She pretty much hated men after that until she met Hottie. But now she knew he wasn't a human man. He was someone from the Other Side.

Chandler instructed Shawna to hold the crystal and the piece of the relic together and call to spirit. The demon was making a lot of noise and protesting, swearing and making threats as the people down there were praying and chanting. Things were flying around in the room they were in, lights switching on and off, doors slamming. When Shawna came down with the tools she needed that it despised and dreaded, it was irate. It screamed bloody murder! It yelled, "Nihil! Nihil! Nihil! Ut auferet meretrex (Go away, whore)!"

The priest said to the demon, "Vos aufera (You go away)!" A storm was brewing outside. There was lightening and crackles of thunder. A big black cloud rolled over Shawna's house.

Shawna put the Selenite crystal inside the piece of Jacob's stone. It sparked as if it were filled with electricity. They fit perfectly as if they were meant to be one piece, not two. She held them in the air, and called out to the lost souls as Chandler told her to. She said, "Come to me. I will show you the way Home!" The wind whipped her hair and gown as if it, itself were protesting her words.

The demon yelled, "Conclusit indigni mortali (Shut up, you unworthy mortal)!"

The priest said, "She is very worthy, you horrible creature! She is in good standing with God! She is doing what he wants her to, of her own free will!"

The demon growled and yelled, "Nihil (No)!"

The priest said, "Hic non habes potestatum (Here, you do not have the power)!"

Then, it hit Kelley. A light bulb went off in her head. "Gatekeeper!" She exclaimed.

"Huic Ostiarius!" yelled the priest.

The Rabbi kept saying the name over and over, rocking as he did so. The spirits began to come. Raina said to Kelley with her eyes closed, "Do you see them?"

Kelley said, "Yes. They're lined up down the street." Paul had stepped aside on the stairs. He was seeing them, too.

"Oh, that's horrible!" said Conor.

"It will do what it has to, to try and deter us from our duties," said Chandler.

"It smells like an outhouse has been overturned in here."

"I know, Conor." The other men in the Order were coughing and choking on the fumes. The demon cackled. "It's taking pleasure in your being bothered by that."

Conor went to the leaded door and beat on it and said, "That smells like crap and flowers. I hate flowers!"

It hissed and cackled more. Then, there was an over powering smell of lavender in the air. They could deal with that. It covered up the awful smell somewhat.

As Shawna repeated her mantra, a great white light appeared in a vortex. The spirits came forth. First was Tracey Paxton. She turned to Shawna and smiled. Shawna said, "Go Home now. Your family's waiting for you." She turned and stepped through the doorway into the light. Then, creepy dead guy showed up. He went into the light, turned around, and smiled. She said, "You were persistent." Many followed who Shawna didn't know.

Then came the man from the Candle Shoppe. He threw his keys to Kelley and said, "It's all yours now, kid," and walked into the light to his wife's awaiting arms.

She said, "Thank you, young lady," to Shawna. The man gave Shawna a grateful nod. Kelley didn't know how to act. She was saddened by the man's passing, yet happy for him, and ecstatic that he gave her the store. She was speechless. She knew she couldn't keep the store, a few years ago, yeah, but not now.

Out of nowhere, up walked Andrew. He said, "I knew it was you." Shawna hugged him and he went Home. There were stragglers. She waited another hour. All the while, the people there repeating their rituals, their mantras to keep the evil one at bay. A demon came down the stairs, threw Paul out of the way since he mistakenly stepped out of the circle to use the downstairs bathroom and resumed his position on the stairs, not taking care to stay in the circle, and charged Shawna. Conor tackled it before Chandler could. They fought. He was able to, with the help of others, overcome the creature, but he didn't move after the fight was over. Kelley started for Conor's body. Chandler got up from his knelt position over Conor's body and told her to stop. He said, "He's gone. Look, Kelley." He pointed to the light, and there stood Conor, smiling. Kelley smiled weakly back at him and cried.

The woman and man, and the other few from the grocery store lot came, too. After the woman from the parking lot crossed over, she was beautiful, around fifty-five, and all cleaned up. She turned and said, "I'm sorry. I didn't mean to scare you. I was only asking for help, trying to tell you that it was you."

Up walked the teacher and others from the school. She nodded to Shawna and walked into the white light. Following up the rear were Cora Mae Simms and her dog Shag. Behind her were Jasper

Rawlins and Kathy Newman. They all crossed over. Kathy was ecstatic to be healthy again.

Chapter 42

An explosive blow jolted the house, followed by the loudest crackle of thunder. It sounded and felt as if a plane had hit the house. There before the people were the Archangels Michael and Gabriel, knelt down where they had landed. The force of their landing gouged a crevasse in the basement floor.

Chandler said, "Thank you both for coming. We're honored." Michael nodded and stared at Chandler, seeming to be telling him something subliminally.

Chandler told Kelley to take Beau outside. With her injuries, she couldn't help anyway. She said, "Come on, buddy. I'm taking you out to potty this time."

Chandler said, "We'll call you when it's safe to bring him back."

She nodded and hurried out.

Chandler yelled, "Get away from that door!" Everyone moved away as Michael pointed at it, forcing the door to cave in on itself. It flew off its hinges.

The evil one had been yelling and cursing prior to their arrival. Now, it was strategizing its next move.

The demon emerged from the room that was its prison for all those years. There it stood, a towering creature with the most wicked sneer on its face. It had no skin, only sinewy muscle over bone, claws for hands, hooves for feet and a tail. Its eyes were as black as the pits of hell.

Crossing herself, the nun gasped at the sight of it. Sulphur filled the air.

The demon glared at Father Martinez and Sister Anna Maria Sanchez and said, "Ut auferet, Sacerdos (Go away, Priest). Et adduxistix in sponsa Christi (And you brought a bride of Christ, too)."

Anna Maria crossed herself again, kissing her rosary beads. The demon laughed. "Serus es, Sacerdos (You're too late, Priest)."

The Angels flanked it on either side, swords drawn. They sliced it everywhere. After each blow, its skin regenerated. Shawna's great uncle Earl' spirit peered out from inside the leaded room and went and looked for his sister upstairs.

Shawna's grandpa's tools, his handsaw, hammer and drill, flew past people's heads. Even screws, bolts, and nails were aimed at the humans, with Shawna as the main target. The Knights were defending Shawna from bolts with their swords like paddles to ping pong balls.

They had formed a human barrier around her.

The Gatekeeper pointed at the priest. Father Martinez's eyes widened as he felt himself floating in the air. Surprised at his levitation, he kicked his legs and waved his arms as if he could swim back down to the ground. He was slammed against the concrete wall. His arms, hands, and feet were punctured by nine-inch nails securing him to the wall.

The nun screamed out in horror at the sight of her friend hung on the wall as Jesus was all those years ago. Sister Anna Maria's screams could hardly be heard over Father Martinez's. Everyone stared in shock at the sight of him nailed to the wall. One final nail flew at the priest and hit him between the eyes. He fell limp. Sister Anna Maria screamed, "No!" and fainted.

That was followed by every screw, bolt and nail that was flying around. They all hit him on his forehead and formed a "crown of thorns" further mocking The Holy Trinity. The demon cackled. Out of respect for the Father and because it was such a terrible, blasphemous sight, seeing him hanging there like our crucified Savior, the Rabbi and Chandler had immediately moved his body by the stairs and covered him in a sheet.

From the crevasse emerged two more demons, one crawling on the wall like a spider, the other slithering on the floor like a snake.

Deep in the crevasse, the Gatekeeper's heir apparent floated in a sulphuric, putrid bath of hatred, evil, foul, ungodly viscous fluid. With every murder, every wicked deed, it grew stronger and was preparing to take its place as successor to the Gatekeeper.

This demon was no fallen Angel. Born of illness, hatred and death, it grew stronger in its putrid stew with the knowledge of its predecessor's battles with the mortals and with the expectation of defeating the next mortal with the power of the one to lift the veil, a descendant of the mortal Shawna, the whore, the dilatory one, its enemy.

As the Archangels fought to take the Gatekeeper down, the other demons prepared to attack the humans. No one noticed the vile creatures as they were concentrating on the Archangels' fight with the Gatekeeper.

However, Declan of the Order did see the one climbing the wall and hurled his sword at it. The blade hit its mark, pinning the demon against the wall where it hung a few feet from where Father Martinez had just been murdered, holy water dripping down the blade tip along with the demon's putrid excretions. The Gatekeeper and the successor's heads both snapped to the side in unison at the dispatching of that demon, both aware now that they were one more short their compendium.

Just as the Gatekeeper turned its head, Saint Michael lopped it off with a mighty swing of his sword. The successor quivered in its mucous-like liquid with anticipation of taking the role as leader of the wicked brigade. It wasn't as strong as it should be yet, but seeing its leader thrown down the crevasse, falling past it, made it burst from its embryonic spew.

At the top of the crevasse, in the basement, Chandler and the men from the Order were surrounding Shawna as she repeated her mantra and soul after soul crossed over.

The other creature that had slithered along the floor entered the deceased father's body. The sheet moved, and Sister Anna Maria was in hysterics, thinking her friend was still alive.

"Ay Dios mio (Oh my God)! Ayúdalo (Help him)!" cried Sister Sanchez. Just then, the Father sat straight up. She went to hug him, and he grabbed her hair, put his mouth to hers, and spit black bile. His corpse fell back to the ground.

Sister Anna Maria laughed a guttural laugh that wasn't her own, ripped off her cross and threw her rosary beads on the ground, and stripped out of her habit and her undergarments. She picked up the crucifix and started masturbating with it in front of all those men, dancing a whore's dance. Her eyes turned a pale white, then solid black, no iris, no sclera. The men couldn't hurt her, as she was merely inhabited by a demon. The Rabbi went to her and started chanting in Latin. A deep voice came from the sister, unlike her sweet, reserved one. "Fuck me, Rabbi," she growled. After that, she gyrated her hips and vagina in front of his face. He could smell the nun's femininity, yet it was mixed with the foul odor of the demon. That repelled the Rabbi. Nun or not, she was a sight to behold, a naked virginal beauty dancing there in front of all of them to see. No modesty in her eyes now, only lust. If the men hadn't had their wits about them, they might have succumbed to her seduction. That is, until the monster's true identity was revealed.

After not getting the response from Rabbi Durst it had hoped for, Sister Anna Maria's face changed.

Her mouth had been torn under her nose, down her chin and at the corners. Her lips had formed into a labia, her mouth a vulva with gnashing teeth, a clitoris under her nose. The demon suckled it smiling revealing a double row of jagged teeth between slurps. Wrinkles between her eyes and around them and horns jutting out from beneath her hair transformed this beautiful girl into the monster's true form.

They were all aghast at the sight of this gentile woman exhibiting such repulsive behavior, and if it wasn't bad enough that the poor girl's modesty had been compromised, the creature was violating the poor woman with whatever it could find. She cackled maniacally. The few men who had initially just stared at her body snapped out of it. They flanked her, a man on each arm and leg, and held her down and as she protested, they poured Holy water down her throat. The Rabbi blessed her with olive oil, the oil of our people. The Monk threw salt over her shaking his ceremonial stick at the demon and chanting in his native tongue. The creature screamed in pain shaking its head back and forth so quickly the men holding it down couldn't see a face anymore.

In a last attempt to injure, a clawed hand reached out for the monk's face as he looked away taking care to not make eye contact with the creature. It just missed him. The demon inhabiting Anna Maria melted into the concrete underneath her.

They helped her to her knees, and Sister Anna Maria vomited. She attempted to wretch up the unholiness that had invaded her purity, but it had left her body. Now, she vomited because she was sickened by the ordeal her body had been put through, and out of embarrassment. The poor girl cried and was mortified when she realized she was naked. She screamed when the cross fell out of her. Sympathizing with her, the Rabbi comforted her as she grabbed for her habit to cover herself. Chandler was there with a blanket to cover her up. Anna Maria did not look up. She couldn't make eye contact with anyone in the room. She silently prayed for strength, asking for forgiveness. Following Raina, Rabbi Durst walked Sister Anna Maria upstairs to Shawna's shower, the monk following them all throwing salt over his shoulder. The men waited outside Shawna's room as Raina helped the traumatized girl into a hot shower.

That was enough of a distraction for the Successor to crawl up the craggy walls and climb out of the crevasse and hide.

After Michael and Gabriel had thrown the Gatekeeper down the pit, they walked over to the vortex to the Other Side. Chandler said, "Thank you." The others echoed his response to their coming. Michael turned around and pointed at the smoldering crevasse. It immediately sealed up, as if there had never been a trauma to the floor, as if nothing evil had ever come from the benign, gray cement. The last of the spirits that had lined up outside had crossed over.

Chandler went and got Kelley and Beau. As Kelley entered the basement, she collapsed from internal bleeding. Shawna ran to her side. She held Kelley's hand. Chandler bent down to help her up. She whispered, "Bathroom." Chandler walked her to the entrance to the downstairs bathroom and she said, "No!" He understood then that she didn't want to go in there.

Pointing to the bathroom, Chandler said, "Declan!" The man walked to the bathroom door, followed by four others from the Order. Declan opened the door, and they saw why Kelley had not wanted to go in there. She had known that something evil was in there.

Declan entered the bathroom with the other men and found the Successor with its bones still fusing together. There were snapping noises as each vertebra locked into place. Its skin was fusing around the bones when the men grabbed it. The creature struggled to get out of their grip to no avail. They had no crevasse to throw it back into so the men carried it to the room with the leaden door.

The demon's skin had completely generated around its skeletal structure. It was strong enough to stand by the time they had gotten it to the door. It gathered its strength. With its sole purpose in mind, it tore Declan's arm off and threw the other men off of itself. They all fell backward as it burst out of their grip, Declan's arm still in its clawed grasp.

The women looked away. The men charged it. With all their might, they pushed it inside the room, unaware that Declan was behind it and flew with the creature's body into the room behind the evil being.

The Order started for their friend, but he shouted, "Close the door!"

"Are you mad man?" shouted Shamus.

On his knees, clutching his shoulder where his arm used to be Declan screamed, "Shut the damn door!"

Saddened and shocked, Shamus of the Order picked up Declan's sword and closed the door with the help of Chandler and the other men. Shamus hung his head, sniffed, wiped his eyes and straightened his shoulders. Just then, Raina had come back downstairs leaving the sister to her privacy and the rabbi and monk upstairs guarding the doorway for her.

The demon smiled a wicked sneer as it approached Declan.

From within, they heard Declan's horrific screams. Tears were seen on some of the other men's faces.

Down the stairs came Jess and Gussy. He walked up to Shawna. Pearl joined him. Jess said to Shawna, "Missy, this is my Missus. I guess that makes me your great, great, great uncle." Shawna hugged them both. Up walked Earl, Pearl's brother. Pearl hugged him, calling him an old fool for locking himself in that room with the creature. Earl hugged her back. "Hush now, gal. I'm fine. I'm with you now."

They all crossed over then.

Kelley started for the vortex where Conor stood waiting for her smiling.

"Kelley?"

Kelley looked at Shawna and answered her. "Uterine cancer. It's metastasized. I'd rather go now while I have the opportunity than when it gets worse."

"Why didn't you tell me?"

"Why? So you could worry too?" Shawna cried and hugged Kelley. Kelley broke the hug and moved toward Raina, handing her the keys to the Candle Shoppe. "It's yours now," she said. "It's Instant Karma on Main Street." She turned around to face Chandler and opened her arms. He walked over to her expecting just a hug. They embraced. She kissed him passionately. He didn't pull away from her. Shawna chuckled. Kelley then said, "Chandler, you have no idea how long I've been wanting to do that!" Shawna giggled again. Chandler blushed. Smiling, she walked into the light and was embraced by her Nana and stood waiting for Shawna and Beau. Kelley picked up the real Fidget and snuggled him.

Paul asked, "Is it over? Shawna said yes. He walked over to Shawna, grabbed her hand to leave with her. She didn't walk with him. He turned and looked at her quizzically. She said, "I have to go with them, and said goodbye to Paul. His eyes watered, he asked, "Why?"

"Because I promised I would. We'll see each other soon."

"But."

"I have to go Paul."

"Well, I'm going with you then." Shawna shook her head no trying to pull away from him.

"It's not your time Paul, nor your destiny." said Chandler.

"But I should be able to go if Kelley is!" retorted Paul.

No Paul. I'll see you when you do cross over but, now you have to go on with your life without me. He was very upset by her words. Looking down, he scratched his head and wiped his eyes and nose.

Paul hugged her. "I'll never forget you." Shawna mouthed goodbye to Paul as she walked away. Disappointed, he gave her a small wave goodbye and hung his head to hide his tears.

She said to Beau, "Come on, baby. Let's go home."

Chandler said, "I'll be with you before you know it sweetheart."

Shawna blew him a kiss and mouthed, "I love you."

Chandler put his hand to his heart, then pointed at her with the other. She smiled.

Shawna and Beau walked into the light after Kelley crossed over.

Jess, Gussy, Pearl, Earl, Kelley, Nana and Conor were waiting for her and Beau. The two dogs caught up with Shag and all the other dogs on The Other Side and ran through a beautiful meadow together ahead of Shawna and the others, all young, healthy, whole and happy once again.

The vortex closed.

Reluctantly, Paul left. He and Raina walked to the Robin's Nest for coffee, cocoa for Paul and closure.

The End

Epilogue

30 years later

Siara Livingston was out planting flowers in her backyard. She had just finished with the last row of bulbs she was putting in that day. She took off her gloves, slapped them on her jeans, and called her dog to go inside for some water. "Barkley, come on!" He came running from next door with the neighbor dogs, Beau and Gussy. "Hey guys," she said. Up walked her neighbors, Kelley and Shawna. They came over for morning coffee as they had every day since Siara had moved in. Shawna brought a cherry pie. Siara said, "Funny you should bring that. The neighbors across the street came over yesterday and introduced themselves with a cherry pie. Their names are Raina and Paul. Do you guys know them?"

"We've met," said Shawna. She looked at Kelley. She smiled. They all went inside, the dogs too.

Kelley said, "Here Siara, I found this in your yard on our way over. It's selenite." Siara took the rock from Kelley and said how pretty it was. Kelley said, "Keep it. It might bring you luck."

"I do like it," said Siara.

"Good." Shawna and Kelley grinned at each other.

There was a banging coming from downstairs. Siara said, "I don't know what that is, but I've been hearing it a lot lately." The dogs ran toward the noise. The three of them followed. They were all on the landing when Siara thought she saw a man in white carrying a candle walking in front of that door she so often heard that noise coming from. She thought she saw her neighbors looking at the man, too, but she thought, *they would tell me if they thought they saw him too. Wouldn't they?*

Kelley said, "Mmmmm." Shawna elbowed her. Kelley quickly said, "That pie sounds good right now."

Barkley barked, but Beau and Gussy didn't bark at the apparition they knew all too well. Siara said, "Come on guys, let's go back upstairs. Silly dog!"

About the Author

Kimberley is a mom and a grandma. She is formerly from Rockford, Illinois. She lives in Wisconsin with her two dogs, Zeiger (Ziggy) and Teddy Doo Doo. She's had her fair share of paranormal experiences in her lifetime. She says that she has become more aware of her spiritual gifts as the years have passed, and that we all possess them. Some people are more open to them than others are. There's a book following this one where she'll share her experiences. She will tell many people's stories of their encounters with ghosts and spirits, along with her own paranormal encounters. The book will also include UFO sightings and other phenomena. You can search for it by author.

A Note to My Readers

Many of Kelley's and Shawna's experiences in this book have been my own, with the exception of the priest and Nana. I have *never* played with a Ouija board or touched a deck of Tarot cards, let alone gotten a card reading, and I will *never* do any of those things. I studied Tarot online so I could write knowledgeably about it.

We are all clairaudient, clairsentient, and clairvoyant to a certain degree. That's your sixth sense. Some people are more attuned to these phenomena. Because I am one of those people, I was troubled as a child by paranormal experiences. My gift is more finely tuned than the average person's, and I'm sure, not as well as others. Some people completely ignore them or scoff at the idea of having a sixth sense, but you cannot deny when you have a feeling that something's not right about someone or something and your "intuition" is right. You just had that feeling! That's your sixth sense. I know what people are thinking a lot of the time. I have precognitive dreams. It's a lot to deal with. It was, especially when I was young. Now, I've come to terms with my "gifts".

You can read about my real-life ghost stories in one of my next books about spirits, ghost stories, and hauntings. It will include a lot of other people's spiritual encounters and ghost stories and my recent near-death experience, and possibly other people's near-death experiences, along with U.F.O. sightings.

I grew up living across the street from a cemetery, so you can imagine how busy my social calendar was, spiritually speaking. I believe the cemetery was moved to make way for a road and only the headstones were moved, not the bodies laid to rest there. Mind you, this all occurred prior to that movie with the same story line. Houses were built there, and the one I lived in felt it was at the center of it all. I have been in most every other house in the near vicinity and never experienced anything paranormal there. It's like my character Kelley says, "Our lights shine brighter than most people's. We're like beacons in the night to the spiritually lost."

Made in the USA
Lexington, KY
26 May 2019